T·H·E
GREENHOUSE

T·H·E
GREENHOUSE

AUDUR AVA OLAFSDOTTIR
TRANSLATED BY Brian FitzGibbon

amazon crossing

The Greenhouse by Audur Ava Olafsdottir was first published in 2009 by Salka Forlag in Reykjavik as *Afleggjarinn*.

Translated from the Icelandic by Brian FitzGibbon.
First published in English in 2011 by AmazonCrossing.

Published by AmazonCrossing
P.O. Box 400818
Las Vegas, NV 89140

ISBN-13: 9781611090796
ISBN-10: 1611090792
Library of Congress Control Number: 2011904667

Dedicated to my mother

"And God said, Behold, I have given you every herb bearing seed, which is upon the face of all the earth, and every tree, in the which is the fruit of a tree yielding seed."—Genesis 1:29

One

Because I'm leaving the country and it's difficult to know when I'll be back, my seventy-seven-year-old father is preparing a memorable last supper for me and is going to cook something from one of Mom's handwritten recipes, the kind of thing Mom might have cooked on such an occasion.

—I was thinking of having fried haddock in breadcrumbs, he says, followed by cocoa soup with whipped cream.

I pick Jósef up from the care center in the seventeen-year-old Saab while Dad tries to sort out the cocoa soup. Jósef is standing eagerly on the sidewalk and clearly happy to see me. He's in his Sunday best because I'm leaving, wearing the last shirt Mom bought him, violet with a pattern of butterflies.

While Dad is frying the onions and the fish lies waiting on a bed of breadcrumbs, I stroll out to the greenhouse to fetch the rose cuttings I'm taking with me. Dad follows me at a distance with the scissors to get some chives to put on the haddock. Jósef follows silently in his footsteps but has stopped entering the greenhouse since he saw the broken glass after the February storms, when several windows were smashed. Instead he stands outside by the mounds of snow, observing us. He and Dad are wearing the same waistcoats, hazel brown with golden diamonds.

—Your mother used to put chives on her haddock, says Dad, and I take the scissors from him, bend over an evergreen bush in a corner of the greenhouse, trim the tips off the chives, and hand them to him. I'm the sole heir to Mom's greenhouse, as Dad frequently reminds me. Though it's hardly a vast plantation; we're not talking about three hundred and fifty tomato plants and fifty cucumber trees that have been passed down from mother to son here, just the rosebushes that pretty much take care of themselves and about ten remaining tomato plants, maybe. Dad is going to do the watering while I'm away.

—I was never really into greens, lad, that was more your mother's thing. One tomato a week is about all I can stomach. How many tomatoes do you think these plants will yield?

—Try to give them away then.

—I can't be constantly knocking on neighbors' doors with tomatoes.

—What about Bogga?

I say this knowing full well that Mom's age-old friend probably shares Dad's limited palate for food.

—You don't honestly expect me to go visiting Bogga with three bags of tomatoes every week? She'd insist on me staying for dinner.

I know what's coming next.

—I would've liked to have invited the girl and the child, he continues, but I knew you'd be against it.

—Yeah, I'm against it; me and the girl, as you call her, are not a couple and never have been, even though we have a child together. It was an accident.

I've already explained myself perfectly clearly and Dad must surely realize that the child is the result of a moment's carelessness, and that my relationship with its mother lasted one quarter of a night, not even, a fifth, more like it.

—Your mother wouldn't have been against inviting them to your last dinner.

Every time Dad needs to add weight to his words, he summons Mom from the grave to get her opinion.

I feel a bit odd now that I'm standing here on the spot of the conception, if I can call it that, with my aging father standing beside me and my mentally challenged twin brother on the other side of the glass.

Dad doesn't believe in coincidences, or at least not when it comes to major events in life such as birth and death. A life doesn't just start or end out of pure chance, he says. He just can't get his head around the fact that conception can be the result of a fluke encounter, that a man can suddenly find himself in bed with a woman without warning, no more than he can understand that death can be the simple consequence of loose wet gravel on a bend, because there are so many other factors for him to consider, figures and numerical calculations. Dad looks on these things differently; the world is a cluster of numbers that hang together, making up the innermost core of creation, and the interpretation of dates can yield profound truths and beauty. The things I just call coincidence or chance, depending on circumstances, are all part of some intricate system for Dad. Too many coincidences can't be discarded as chance, one maybe, but not three, not three in a row, he says: Mom's birthday, his granddaughter's birthday, and the day of Mom's death, all on the same date—August the seventh. Personally, I don't understand Dad's calculations. In my experience, as soon as you think you've got one thing figured out, something completely different happens. I've got nothing against the pastimes of a retired electrician, so long as his calculations do not interfere with my careless use of contraception.

—You're not running away from anything, lad?

—No. I said good-bye to the girls yesterday, I add.

He knows he won't get any further with me on this one so he changes subject.

—You don't happen to know where your mother hid her cocoa soup recipe, do you? I bought some whipping cream.

—No, but maybe we can try to figure it out together.

Two

When I come back from the greenhouse, Jósef is sitting totally upright at the table with his hands on his lap, wearing his red tie and violet shirt. My brother takes a lot of interest in clothes and colors and, like Dad, always wears a tie. Dad has two hot plates going at once, one for the pot of potatoes, the other for the frying pan. Not that he seems to be fully in control of the cooking; maybe he's nervous because I'm leaving. I rummage around him and pour some oil into the pan.

—Your mother always used margarine, he says.

Neither of us is particularly apt at cooking. My role in the kitchen was mainly limited to loosening the lids of red cabbage jars and applying the can opener to cans of peas. Actually Mom used to make me wash up and Jósef dry. But he took ages on each plate so in the end I'd snatch the tea cloth off him and finish the drying myself.

—You're not likely to be getting much haddock over the coming months, Lobbi lad, says Dad. I don't want to hurt his feeling by telling him that, after my four-month stint of handling fish at sea, I don't care if I never eat a single morsel of fish again.

Because Dad is determined to give his boys a treat, he surprises us with a curry sauce.

—I followed a recipe I got from Bogga, he says.

The sauce has a peculiar but beautiful green color, like shimmering grass after a spring shower. I ask him about the color.

—I used curry and some food coloring, he explains. I notice he's taken a jar of rhubarb jam and placed it beside my plate.

—That's the last jar of your mother's jam, he says, and I watch his shoulders as he stirs the sauce in his brown diamond-patterned waistcoat.

—You're not going to have rhubarb jam with the fish though?

—No, I just thought you might like to take the jar with you on your journey.

My brother Jósef is silent, and Dad doesn't say much at the table either, so the three of us don't make a very talkative bunch, really. I serve my brother and cut his two potatoes in two for him. He obviously doesn't like the look of the green sauce and meticulously scrapes it off the fish, pushing it to one side of his plate. I look at my brown-eyed brother, who bears an eerie resemblance to a famous movie star. There's no way of knowing what's going through his head. To atone for his sins and strike some balance at the table, I take an ample helping of Dad's sauce. It's at around this time that I feel the pain in my stomach for the first time.

After dinner, while I'm washing up, Jósef makes some popcorn, as he normally does when he visits on weekends. He fetches the usual big pot in the cupboard, measures exactly three tablespoons of oil, and carefully sprinkles the contents of the packet into the pot until the yellow corn covers the bottom. Once that's done, he places the lid on the pot and puts the plate on at full heat for four minutes. Then, when the oil begins to simmer, he lowers the heat down to two. He grabs the glass bowl and salt and doesn't take his eyes off the pot for a single moment until the task has been completed. Then the three of us watch *Newsnight*. My brother holds my hand on the sofa; the glass bowl is on the table. An hour and a half into my twin brother's weekend visit, he hands me the CD with the songs. It's dancing time.

✳

Three

I'm taking very little with me, and Dad is surprised to see what little luggage I have. I wrap the rose cuttings in moist newspaper and place them in the front compartment of my backpack. We travel in the Saab that has been in Dad's possession for about as long as I can remember. Jósef sits silently in the back. Dad is sporting the beret he always wears on his longer journeys out of town. He's way below the legal speed limit and, since the accident, never goes over twenty-five miles an hour. He's driving so slowly across the rugged lava field that I have time to contemplate the birds perched at regular intervals on the pointed violet crags of the crust of the breaking dawn, for about as far as the eye can see, one after another, like a melancholic musical score mounting in a crescendo. Dad is also unused to driving; Mom did most of that. There is a long trail of cars behind us that are constantly trying to overtake us. Not that my father allows this to distract him. I'm not worried about missing my flight either, because Dad always gets everywhere with plenty of time to spare.

—Would you like me to drive, Dad?

—Thanks for the offer, lad, but no. Just sit back there and take in that landscape you're about to say good-bye to; you're not likely to be driving through lava fields for a while.

We both remain silent for a moment while I take in the landscape I'm saying good-bye to. Later, once we've passed the side road that leads to the lighthouse, Dad wants to chat a little bit about my plans for the future and what I intend to do with my life. He isn't satisfied by my interest in gardening.

—I hope you don't mind your old man asking you a few questions about your plans for the future, Lobbi. I don't mean to be nosy and you know I mean well.

—That's OK.

—Have you made up your mind about what you're going to study?

—I've got a gardening job.

—A man with your academic abilities…

—Don't start, Dad.

—I think you're squandering your talents, son.

It's difficult to explain this to Dad; the garden and roses in the greenhouse were an interest that I shared with Mom.

—Mom would have understood me.

—Yes, your mom pretty much approved of anything you put your mind to, he says. Still, though, she wouldn't have minded if you'd gone to university.

When we first moved into the new neighborhood it was nothing but a flat stretch of barren land with rocks surrounded by wind-scattered pebbles. There were new buildings everywhere, or building sites, half saturated in puddles of yellow water. The low, scraggy bushes didn't come until much later. The neighborhood was exposed to the sea and frequent blasts of wind from which it was impossible to create any shelter in the gardens. People had given up planting flowers in the soil. Mom was the first person who tried to plant trees in the area and, in the early years, was viewed as a bit of an eccentric for attempting the impossible. While others contented themselves with creating lawns or, at the very most, low hedges between the gardens, to be able to bask in the breeze for those three days in the summer, she was out there planting laburnum, maple, ash, and blossoming shrubs on the more shielded side of the house. She never gave up, though, even if she had to plant the scions straight into the rocks.

The second summer Dad built a greenhouse south of the house. We first placed the plants in the greenhouse and then took them out into the garden in the first or second week of June when there was no longer any frost at night. Initially we were only going to keep them outside for the summer and then move them back into the greenhouse, but eventually, if there was a mild autumn, we'd prolong their stay outside by another month or so. Then one winter we even let our plants rest under a six-and-a-half-foot-high blanket of snow. In the end there was nothing that wouldn't grow in Mom's garden; everything seemed to blossom in her hands. Bit by bit, the patch grew into a fairy-tale garden that attracted attention and wonderment. Since Mom's death, the women in the neighborhood have sometimes asked me for advice. It just needs a little bit of care and, most of all, time, my mother would have said—that was pretty much her gardening philosophy in a nutshell.

—I admit you and your mother had your own world that Jósef and I weren't a part of; maybe we didn't understand it.

Lately Dad has been referring to himself and Jósef as a unit— Jósef and myself, he says.

Mom sometimes felt an urge to go out and work in the garden or greenhouse in the heart of midsummer nights. It was as if she didn't need to sleep the way other people did, especially in the summer. When I'd come home in the early hours after a night out with my friends, there would be Mom on the flower bed with her red plastic bucket and pink floral gardening gloves while Dad was fast asleep inside. Naturally there wasn't a soul in sight, and everything was so incredibly still. Mom would say hi and look at me as if she knew something about me that I didn't. Then I would sit beside her in the grass for a few quarters of an hour and pull up some weeds as a token gesture, just to keep her company. I might have had half a bottle of beer in my hand, which I'd prop up in the flower bed while I lie down, rest my chin in the palms of my cupped hands and gaze at the drifting puffs of cloud. Whenever I wanted to be alone with Mom, I went out to her in the greenhouse or in the garden; that's where we could talk together. Sometimes she'd seem distracted and I'd ask her what she was thinking and she'd just say, "Yeah, yeah, I like what you're saying." And then she'd give me an approving and encouraging smile.

—There's no great future in gardening for a brilliant student like you.

—Since when am I a brilliant student?

—I might be old, lad, but I'm not senile. It so happens that I've kept all your exam results. Top of the class at the age of twelve. Top of your year at the age of sixteen, graduating with flying colors.

—I can't believe you keep that stuff. It was on top of a box somewhere in the basement. Throw that garbage away, Dad.

—Too late, Lobbi, I've asked Þröstur to frame it for me.

—You're not serious?

—So are you thinking of a university degree then?

—No, not at the moment.

—How about botany?

—No.

—Biology?

—No.

—Then how about plant physiology or plant genetics with an emphasis on plant biotechnology?

Dad has obviously been reading up on this stuff. He keeps both hands firmly gripped on the wheel with his eyes glued to the road.

—No, I've no interest in being a scientist or a university lecturer.

I'm much more in my element when I'm in wet soil. It's so different to be able to touch living plants; lab flowers don't give off any smell after a shower of rain. It's difficult to put Mom's and my world into words for Dad. My interest is in what grows out of fertile soil.

—Still, I want you to know that I've set up a little fund you can use if you want to continue your education and go to university. That's apart from your mother's inheritance money. Jósef is happy where he is, he adds. Of course, I'll make sure he's not short of anything.

—Thank you.

I don't discuss the gardening any further with Dad. How can I tell the electrician that I might not even know what I want? How difficult it can be to make a decision like that, once and for all, at a specific point in one's life?

—You won't get far on dreams, Lobbi, Dad would say.

—You've got to follow your dreams, Mom would have said. And then she would have gazed out the kitchen window, as if she were surveying a vast dominion, and not just those few yards to the greenhouse and another few again to the fence. The entire garden was a single plot of swarming vegetation, and it was impossible to see beyond the fences through the rich tangle of plants, trees, and bushes; but it was almost as if she half expected guests from far away. Then she would empty the bag of prunes into a bowl, place it under the tap, and let water run over it.

—It certainly beats being seasick on a small boat for months on end, Dad finally says.

Four

We continue to drive through the lava field in silence. I still feel the farewell dinner in my stomach and sense that the nausea that probably started with the green sauce is mutating into a persistent ache, right here in the middle of the lava field, not far from the spot where Mom capsized the car. I know the curve where the car lost control; there's a small basin there overgrown with grass. I can picture the spot where she was cut out of the wreckage quite vividly.

—Your mom shouldn't have gone before me, sixteen years younger, says Dad as we drive past the spot.

—No, she shouldn't have gone before you.

Mom had whims like that, going off to pick blueberries on her birthday at the crack of dawn, to some obscure favorite spot she had; that's why she had to drive across the lava field. Then she was going to offer us—her boys, as she liked to call Dad, Jósef, and me—waffles with freshly picked berries and whipped cream. I realize now that it must have been hard to only have men in the house, not to have had a daughter, I mean.

I give myself some time before I get to Mom in the car, capsized in the lava hollow. I give myself plenty of time to scrutinize the nature and glide around the spot a long moment, like a cameraman on a movie taking an aerial shot from a crane, before I zoom in on Mom herself, the leading lady this whole scene revolves around. It's the seventh of August and I decide to make it an early autumn. That's why I see so much red and glowing golden colors in the nature. I picture nothing but varieties of red at the scene of the accident: russet heather, a bloodred sky, violet red foliage on some small trees nearby, golden moss. Mom herself was in a burgundy cardigan, and the coagulated blood didn't become visible until Dad rinsed it in the bathtub at home. By dwelling on the small details of the set design, like you might look at the backdrop of a painting before shifting your gaze to the main subject itself, I somehow manage to put Mom's death on pause, and therefore postpone the moment of the inevitable farewell. The scene plays out either with Mom still inside the car wreckage, or she's just been cut out and is lying on the ground. I decide that it's on a level plain, the flat base of the lava hollow, as if the tops of two tussocks had been sliced off and grass had been sown on the wound; that's where they very gently lay her down. In my mind she's either still showing some sign of life or she's dead. Dad is driving so slowly that I can check out the tree, which is still there where I planted it, a dwarf pine, my attempt to plant a wood in the middle of a rugged lava field, one isolated tree in the rocky barren landscape; that is how I sanctify Mom's spot.

—Are you cold? Dad asks, turning the heater on full blast. The car's roasting.

—No, I'm not cold.

I do have a pain in my stomach, though, but I don't tell Dad about it. He'd smother me in worries. Mom used to worry in a different way; she understood me.

—Well then, Lobbi lad, we're there now, see the planes?

As soon as we reach the airport, the black blanket begins to lift off the mountain range, uncovering the first rays of dawn below it, like light blue wisps of smoke. The horizontal February sun reveals the dirt on the smudged windshield.

My brother and Dad follow me into the terminal.

Dad hands me a wrapped package as we're saying good-bye.

—You can open it when you land, he says. Just a little something that might remind you of your old man at bedtime.

When I say good-bye to Dad I give him a firm hug, but not a long one, just a brisk embrace and slap him on the back like a man. Then I do the same to my brother, Jósef, who immediately recoils toward Dad and takes his hand. Then Dad takes a fat envelope out of his back pocket and hands it to me.

—I went to the bank and got some cash out for you; you never know what can come up when you're abroad.

I fleetingly glance over my shoulder and see Dad leading my twin brother out of the terminal, Dad's wallet sticking halfway out of his back pocket. They're both in the gray waistcoats that Dad recently bought; it's impossible to say which of the two is the best dressed. Jósef is my total opposite in appearance, short, with brown eyes and dark skin, as if he'd just strolled off a beach. He's so immaculately dressed that, if it weren't for the color combinations of his clothes, my autistic twin brother could be mistaken for an air pilot. In the image I decide to store of him in my mind he is in a violet shirt with butterfly patterns. By the time it's full daylight I will have left this brown slush behind me, and the salt of the earth will only survive in the form of white rings on the rims of my shoes.

Five

It's precisely at the moment when the plane is lifting off the runway and shooting away from the frosty pink snow that I feel a distinct jab of pain in my stomach. I lean over my neighbor to catch a final glimpse through the porthole, of the mountain below, like violet mounds of meat splattered with streaks of white fat. The woman in a yellow polo presses herself back against her seat to give me the full view of her window. But I soon grow tired of measuring her breasts against the string of craters and lose interest in the view. Although I should be feeling lighter, the pain in my gut prevents me from full-heartedly appreciating the sense of freedom that is meant to accompany being above everything that is below. I'm conscious of—rather than actually seeing—the black lava, yellow withered grass, milky rivers, corrugated terrain of tussocks, marshes, fields of wilting lupin, and beyond that an endless stretch of rock. And what could be more hostile than rocks; surely roses can't grow in the middle of broken rocks? This is undoubtedly an extraordinarily beautiful country, and although I'm fond of many things here, both places and people, it's best kept on a stamp.

I stretch into the backpack shortly after takeoff to see how the rose cuttings are faring at an altitude of thirty-three thousand feet. They're still wrapped in the moist newspapers, which I adjust around the green shoots. The fact that I accidentally chose an obituaries page is no doubt apt, considering my current physical state, and also a demonstration of how coincidences can work in subtle ways. At the moment in which I'm detaching myself from the earth below, it's not unnatural to be thinking of death. I'm a twenty-two-year-old man and bound to sink into contemplating death several times a day. Second comes the body, both my own and that of others, and in third place there are the roses and other plants, although the exact order in which I ponder on these three things may vary from day to day. I put the plants down again and sit in the seat beside the woman.

In addition to the pain, which is now turning into a throbbing ache, I feel a mounting nausea and bend over, clutching my stomach. The sound of the engines reminds me of the fishing boat and how nauseous it made me feel in those four months of constant seasickness. I didn't even need a rough sea; the moment I stepped onto the boat my stomach started to surge and I lost all my bearings. As soon as the steel hull started to amplify the sea's vibrations and sway to its rhythm against the wharf, I'd burst into a cold sweat, and by the time we'd raised the anchor, I would already have thrown up once. When I was too seasick to sleep I'd go on deck and peer into the fog, watching the horizon swell up and down, as I tried to steady the waves. After nine fishing trips I was the palest man on the planet; even my eyes were a floating, watery blue.

—That's the snag about being red-haired, the most experienced crewmember had said, they always get the worst seasickness.

—And they rarely come back, said another.

Six

The air hostesses scuttle between the seats; legs in brown nylon stockings and high-heeled mules are now in my direct line of vision as I crouch in a crash-landing position. They've got their eye on me and shuffle up and down the aisle to check on me, dust the fluff off the back of my seat, offer me a pillow and blanket, adjust and rearrange.

—Would you like a pillow, would you like a blanket? they ask with anxious airs, slipping a pillow under my head and throwing a blanket over me. Then they move away again to discuss my case.

—Are you sick? my neighbor in the yellow polo in the window seat asks.

—Yeah, I'm not feeling too good, I say.

—Don't be afraid, she says with a smile, adjusting the blanket over me. I realize now she could be Mom's age. There are three women tending to me on the plane; I'm a little boy on the verge of tears. I stretch in my seat and peer under the tinfoil lid over the tray of food. Then, when a hostess passes, I ask her what was in the meal.

—I'll check, she says and vanishes down the aisle.

She doesn't come straight back, however, and just to show the woman sitting next to me that I'm a well-brought-up fellow, which Mom would certainly confirm, I hold out my hand and introduce myself.

—Arnljótur Thórir.

And better still I dig into my leather jacket and pull out a photograph of a bareheaded infant in a green bodysuit. She might very well be thinking that it isn't very manly of me to be traveling with flower cuttings wrapped in soaked obituaries and to be throwing up the in-flight meal, but I'm not going to give her a chance to ask me any personal questions or even to offer me chocolate, but stay one step ahead of her.

—My daughter, I say, handing her the photograph.

She seems slightly taken aback, but then gives me a friendly smile, fishes her glasses out of her handbag, takes the photograph, and holds it up to the light.

—Pretty child, she says. How old is she?

—Five months old when that picture was taken. Six and a half now, I add. I feel like saying six months and nineteen days, but the pain in my gut won't allow me to dwell on such details.

—A beautiful and intelligent-looking child, she repeats, big bright eyes. She doesn't have a lot of hair for a girl, though, I thought she was a boy, to be honest.

The woman looks at me warmly.

—As far as I remember she'd just woken up and they'd just taken her bonnet off, I say, that's why the hair's like that. Yeah, she was just out of the carriage, I add. I take the picture back and stick it into my pocket. I've nothing to add on the subject of my daughter's lack of hair, so that topic has been exhausted. And this weird pain is rapidly starting to dominate all my thoughts. I have to throw up again, and when I close my eyes I have a flashback of the green sauce over the fried fish. My neighbor looks at me anxiously. I don't have the energy for any further conversation so I pretend I've got other things to be thinking about and rummage through my backpack again. I dig out the book with my collection of dried plants and, as if I were being mocked by fate, immediately stumble upon the page with the oldest plants: the pressed six-leaf clovers, which were all picked on the same morning in our tiny yard back home. Dad thought it was significant that I had found these three six-leaf clovers on my sixth birthday, and saw it as a lucky omen for what lay ahead, at the birthday party later that day maybe, or some dream that would come true, such as a tree growing in the garden for me to climb on.

—Is that a plant collection you've got with you? my female neighbor asks, visibly interested. I don't answer but carefully fish out a clover and hold it up against the reading light; it's the last one that's still intact, delicate and fragile, eternity's flower. I think I'm more than likely suffering from an acute case of food poisoning, but it's no doubt symbolic of the state of my life that the stem of the plant is hanging from a blue thread.

Seven

—Are you sure you'll be all right on your own? the hostess asks me as I walk down the aisle to the exit. You're very pale.

The moment I step off the plane, the head hostess taps me on the shoulder and says:

—We tried to find out what food it was, two of us tasted it, but we're not sure. Sorry. But it's definitely either fish in breadcrumbs with a cream cheese filling or chicken in breadcrumbs with a cream cheese filling.

An airport official writes an address on a slip of paper that I crumple in my clenched clammy palm.

I'm in a city I've never been in before, my very first port of call abroad, and I'm curled up on the backseat of a taxi. The backpack is beside me, and the green shoots pierce through the newspaper wrapping in the top compartment. On second thought, I'm not sure whether I'm alone in the taxi; I can't exclude the possibility that the woman in the yellow polo might have escorted me to my destination.

When the car stops by a sidewalk at a red light I can see people checking their reflections in my window as they pass.

The driver occasionally glances at me through his mirror. He's got a big Alsatian in the front seat with a slavering tongue dangling from its mouth. I can't see whether the dog is on a leash, but his eyes are fixed on me. I close my eyes, and when I open them again, the car has stopped in front of a hospital and the driver has turned around in his seat and is looking at me.

He makes me pay double for having thrown up in his cab, but doesn't look particularly angry; it's more of a scolding air, perhaps, for my irresponsible behavior.

Eight

First, I carefully put down my backpack, making sure the moisture doesn't leak off the rose cuttings. Then I lie down, stretching out on the plastic-covered examination bench. Twenty-two years old and already at the end of the road, the journey's over before it's even started. It takes me a long time to write my name on the form, letter by letter, absolutely ages. The woman who is helping me to lie down in the fluorescent-lit examination room has shiny brown hair as well as brown eyes and is doing everything to assist me. I'm naked down to the waist and am now taking my trousers off. Is this how Mom felt, too, when she was dying out in the lava field in the arms of strangers? At any rate it's clear that the day of my death will be a happy day for many of the inhabitants of this globe; by the time the sun has set, multitudes will have been born in my place and countless wedding feasts will have been held.

Not that dying is any big deal, since almost all of the best sons and daughters of this planet have died ahead of me. Naturally it'll be a blow for my aging father, my autistic twin brother will develop some new system without me, and the as-yet speechless newborn who was still too small to sleep over will never get to know her father. I do have some regrets, mind you. I wish I'd slept around a bit more and planted the rose cuttings in the soil.

When the girl with the shiny hair gently places her hand on my stomach, I notice she's got a green clasp in her hair that's shaped like a butterfly. The woman who is nursing me in the final quarter of an hour of my existence bears the symbol of the continuity of life in her hair.

Rose cuttings can't survive without water, which is why I hoist myself up on my elbows and point at the backpack.

—Plants, I say.

She stoops over the backpack and moves it closer to the bed. I don't even have to know the right words; I point and she's a woman who can understand me. For a moment, I therefore briefly consider whether we might have made a pair, if I hadn't been on my way out of this world, as it were. She could be ten years older, about thirty-two, but right now that doesn't feel like any age gap worth quibbling about. The sinister pain in my gut, however, prevents me from developing this steady relationship of ours any further. When I've finished throwing up the remains of the airplane breadcrumbs and cheese sauce, she helps me to carefully unwrap the moist newspaper from the rose cutting, as if she were removing the bandages around a patient's leg after a successful operation.

—Did you bring plants with you? she asks, and now that she's closer I see that there are yellow dots on the butterfly's wings.

—Yes, I reply in her language with the fluency of a native.

She nods as if I am a man who knows what he's talking about. Then I throw in some Latin for good measure:

—*Rosa candida.*

When it comes to plants and cultivation, my performance and vocabulary both expand considerably. Then I add:

—Without thorns.

—Without thorns, really? she says, folding my jeans and placing them tidily on the chair, over my blue cable-knit sweater, the last sweater Mom knit for me. In a moment's time the woman with a butterfly hair clip will also be the last of seven women to have seen me naked.

—And are the other two plants also—she hesitates—*Rosa candida?*

—Yes, for safety, I say, to produce offspring, just in case one of them dies, I say, allowing myself to slip back onto the plastic mattress again.

Since she has already been witness to my suffering, and helped me to throw up and water the rose cuttings, I feel the urge to share something more personal with her. Which is why I pull out the photo of my child and hand it to her.

—My daughter, I say.

She takes the picture and scrutinizes it.

—Cute, she says and smiles at me. How old is she?

She asks simple and manageable questions that my grasp of the language can easily handle.

—About seven months.

—Very cute, she repeats, but not much hair for a seven-month-year-old girl maybe.

This I had not been expecting. You place your trust in another person's hands, sharing something important with them in that final moment, and they let you down. All of a sudden I feel it's vital that the last person I communicate with in this life should understand this hair thing once and for all. That photographs can be deceiving and that hair on blond children isn't particularly visible in the first year, that there's no comparison to dark-haired children who are normally born with a lot of hair. There's a lot I'd like to get off my chest, and it's only my pain and limited linguistic skills that are preventing me from defending my daughter.

—About seven months, I repeat, as if this definitively explained the lack of hair. Then I realize it was a bit rash of me to show her the photograph and I no longer want her to be fidgeting with it.

—Give it to me, I say abruptly, stretching out my hand to take the picture back. I look at Flóra Sól, my daughter, grinning with two teeth in her lower gum, and remember in fact seeing her with a small curl of hair over her forehead, fresh out of the bath, when I came to say my good-byes to her and her mother without ringing ahead of me.

I close my eyes as I'm wheeled into the operating theater and feel cold under the sheet. Pain is the only tangible reality I can cling to right now, although my suffering obviously pales into insignificance when compared to the mutilations and horrors of this world, droughts, hurricanes, and warfare.

I try to gauge my chances of survival in the expressions and gestures of the people dressed in green. Someone says something to someone else, who laughs heartily behind a green mask; it's not as if there's anything serious going on here, not as if anyone's about to die. There could be nothing more crushing in my final moments than to be subjected to the flippancy of this motley crew, the careless, slapdash attitudes of those who'll still be here once I'm gone. They aren't even talking about me—as far as I can make out—but some movie that one of them went to see and that someone else is going to see tonight. *The Poppy Field*, yeah, I've heard about that movie, it's about a man who's badly rejected and kidnaps the woman who rejected him and then they rob a bank together; the movie recently won some special award at a film festival.

Suddenly someone briskly strokes my hair. My ginger mop of hair, Mom would have said.

—Don't worry, it's your appendix, someone says behind a mask.

Strokes isn't really the right word. It's more as if someone were briskly running their fingers through my hair. I'm a bird and take off with heavy flapping wings. Hovering in midair above, I follow what's going on below but take no part in it, because I'm free from all things. In the instant before everything fades I feel I can hear Dad beside me:

—There's no future in roses, Lobbi boy.

Nine

When I wake up I don't immediately remember where I am. For a moment I feel I catch a whiff of wet soil and vegetation, like waking up in a tent in the rain, and yet everything is white. I'm all alone in the room, which my eyes scan before settling on the bedside table beside me. Three green stalks have been placed in as many plastic glasses; I recognize them, they're my rose cuttings. A handwritten note has been squeezed between them. I reach under the covers to grope the body that has been cut open and patched up to make sure it's real, that I'm still alive. I check my pulse and then feel a heartbeat. I move farther down and gently stroke my stomach muscles, once clockwise, and also take the time to investigate other parts of the body. Finally I reach the bandaged spot where I was operated on and gently press the wound. Then I hoist myself up on my elbows and, despite my light-headedness and the stretch on my stitches, manage to fish out my dictionary from the top pocket of the backpack. It takes a while to decipher the whole message, word by word: *I took care of your rose cuttings and passed the word on to my colleague in the next shift. Am taking time off to visit my parents in the country. Speedy recovery, red-haired boy. P.S. Found Christmas package in the backpack when I was checking the plants.*

She's left the package from Dad on top of the quilt. It's wrapped in Christmas gift paper with reindeer and bell patterns and a curled blue ribbon.

I open the package. It's a pair of pajamas, thick flannel pajamas with long, light blue stripes. They look like Dad's stripy pajamas and those he bought for my brother Jósef. I take them out of the plastic and remove the cardboard. Dad has removed the price tag. As I lift the pajama top up, a handwritten card falls out of one of the sleeves:

Lobbi lad. There is much to be remembered and to be thankful for over the past year. Jósef and myself send you our warmest regards and hope that these unpretentious pajamas will come in useful in those "perilous storms" (his quotation marks on the card) they have overseas.

Yours, Dad and Jósef.

He has even got Jósef to scrawl his initials underneath. What did he mean by "unpretentious"? He knows I normally sleep in my underpants; is it pretentious to sleep without pajamas the way I do?

I'm going to get out of bed in my bare feet, but the stitches hurt and I feel dizzy. I feel how heavy I am, as if I were up to my knees against a strong current, so I lie down again and doze off.

When I wake up again there's a woman in a white coat standing by my bed, with long brown hair tied in a ponytail, but she's not the same one as the last time. I get some sweetened teabag tea to drink and a slice of toast with cheese. She talks to me, as I drink the tea, and shows some interest in the plants.

—What species is this? she asks.

I choose words that are befitting to this new lease on life.

—Eight-petaled roses, I say, in an unrecognizable, husky voice.

—Are they all the same species?

—Yes, two of them are extra cuttings, in case one dies, to produce some offspring, I say with a thick tongue and in this stranger's voice; my body and voice don't seem to match anymore.

—Your voice will soon come back to you, she says, that's the anesthetic.

I'm incredibly sleepy and feel I'm dropping off again, as if I can neither shake off my dreams nor stay awake.

The next time I wake up there are two people in white coats standing on either side of my bed talking to each other. One of them lifts up the duvet on my bandaged side, and although I manage to grasp a few words here and there, they're talking fast and I can't place the sentences in any context. I'm still finding it difficult to stay awake. They're talking about me, asking me about something, and as I try to formulate an answer I start to fade again, dozing off mid-conversation.

—He's out of it, let's just let him sleep, is the last thing I hear.

Because I regularly fall asleep when people try to talk to me, I get to stay two days longer in the hospital. No one makes any remarks about the rose cuttings; each new shift seems to be filled in and I'm allowed to keep them in peace.

Every time I doze off I have the same dream. I dream I'm in new and pretty good blue Wellingtons and that I'm working in a famous and remote rose garden. I have a clear picture of the boots as I awaken; they're probably one size too big. Nothing else is in color in the dream, not even the roses, just the blue boots. Then the dream takes a sudden twist, which I'm forced to follow. Looking down a narrow alley, I see Mom standing at the end of it, silhouetted against the light. I follow her in the blue boots up a long staircase and to a door she disappears behind. I knock on the door and she comes to it. She offers me teabag tea with sugar.

When I finally wake up properly, I've missed three days on the calendar. Now that I'm alive again there are countless options open to me. Because I wake up in a sweat after the dream, the nurse who is on duty on my last morning at the hospital wants me to have a shower before I check out. I follow her to the bathroom, taking one short step at a time because the stitches hurt.

This one has brown eyes, too, but short brown hair. I would have preferred to be left alone, but she stands there watching me, in case something happens to me, I suppose; there's no denying that the women who have been looking after me have shown great care. I shed my hospital clothes and place them on a chair in front of the bathroom mirror. When I step out of the shower she has already wiped the steam off the mirror. I contemplate my mortal flesh as she changes the bandage on the right-hand side of my stomach. Black bristles protrude from the skin. Right now, the moment after I've stepped out of the shower with the nurse on my left-hand side, I feel like I'm nothing more than this new body with a scar. Feelings, memories, and dreams no longer make me what I am, but I'm first and foremost a male body made of flesh and blood. Having experienced death and resurrection and communicated with three brown-eyed nurses in as many days, I graduate from the hospital and am given a box with four pink painkillers to take home with me.

I get dressed and pack the rose cuttings back into my backpack along with the plant collection and pajamas. When I dig into the backpack in search of a clean T-shirt to put on, I find Mom's last jar of rhubarb jam, which Dad stuck in there. The nurse hands me a few sheets of newspaper to wrap around the plants, and I immediately notice they're theater reviews.

—Do you have anyone to go to? the doctor who checks me out asks.

I tell him I'll be in good hands.

The only challenge I face in this life right now is zipping up the fly on my jeans. I do my best to fend for myself and manage to slip into my pants unassisted, but I'm sore around the wound, and in the end the brown-eyed woman comes to my rescue.

✹

Ten

I ring Dad from a phone booth on the way out of the hospital. I clear my throat several times while the phone is ringing and tell him as nonchalantly as possible that I unexpectedly had to have my appendix out. I do my best to strike a casual tone, but my voice is all husky and weird, as if some total stranger had stepped in to dub the first chapters of this brief autobiographical film of my life, and all of a sudden I'm almost crying.

Dad wants me to come home on the next plane. When I tell him it's out of the question, he wants to fly out himself and take care of me while I'm recovering. I can hear he's worried.

—Your mother would have wanted that, he says. Actually I've been wanting to take Jósef abroad for some time, he adds. He likes flying.

I tell him how things are, that I've been loaned an apartment.

—A student's cubbyhole way up on the sixth floor, with no elevator.

—Well then, Jósef and I will just stay at the inn.

He talks like someone out of an old book, as if there were only one inn in the entire city. As if they half expected to be given no shelter because the guesthouse would be full and they'd have to sleep in a barn.

It takes me a good while to convince my father, who is just three years away from being eighty and on the point of hopping on a plane with his handicapped son, that I don't need anyone to take care of me. I struggle to revive my voice and tell him not to worry, that I'm going to be staying with my friend who is studying archaeology here.

—You remember Thórgun, I say, the girl who was in my class for the whole of primary school and often came home with me, the one who played the cello, with glasses and braces.

She was also actually in secondary school with me, too, but had stopped coming home with me by then. Then I'd bumped into her in a flower shop when she was back in the country on vacation; I needed some fertilizer and she held a viola cornuta. On the way out she informally invited me to come over and stay with her.

—It's a very nice apartment she has, I now say, having previously given him the impression that it was a student slum—I'll be quick to recover there. She'll definitely cook for me, I quickly add to appease my father, who's always protective of his twins, his only children. What I don't tell him is that the archaeology student is, in fact, away for a week, looking at graveyards in two towns and broadening her horizons.

—You can always come home, he says. I haven't touched anything in your room, it's just as you left it, except that I tidied it up a bit, changed the sheets, and mopped the floor. It took me a whole evening to iron the sheets.

—We've been through all that, Dad. I'll be here for a few days more until the stitches are removed, then I'm buying a second-hand car and driving down south to the garden, which will take me a good few days.

I can feel how tired I am and simply don't have the stamina for a long dialogue. Although I've yet to thank him for the pajamas. Winding the conversation down requires both concentration and energy.

—Thanks for the pajamas, they came in very handy.

Then I give Dad the phone number of my old confirmation mate—as he calls her—who is lending me her bed while she's away digging up two graveyards with a trowel and gaining some experience that will presumably be a revelation to her and broaden her vision of the world. He says he's going to call me again this evening to find out how I've managed.

It isn't far to my friend's place, but the stitches hurt when I walk. As I'm walking there, I take in the buildings and the people. Most of the women definitely have brown hair and brown eyes.

The keys are in the bakery on the ground floor, although the apartment itself is on the sixth floor at the top, a loft, and no elevator. There are four keys in the bunch, and the woman in the bakery explains to me what each one is for: one for the hall door downstairs, the others for the cellar, mailbox, and my friend's apartment. The staircase creaks; each step is a challenge for my newly stitched wound. The apartment is cold, but everything is clean and well ordered. The bed has been neatly made, and I'm assuming that under the bedspread there is the duvet that I've been loaned for a week, while my schoolmate, whom I've actually lost all contact with, investigates tombstones. It's obvious that a female lives here; it's full of small, unnecessary objects, candlesticks, lace tablecloths, incense, cushions, books, and pictures I have to be careful not to bump into. She's obviously bought everything in an antiques market. The nano apartment has an antique desk on which there is an antique lamp, and then there's an antique bed, antique candlesticks, and an antique mirror in the hallway in which I catch my reflection as I enter.

The height of the mirror is clearly intended for a female of average height, and I have to bend over considerably to be able to contemplate myself.

I run my hand though my thick, bristly hair, one of my striking characteristic gestures. There is no question about it: I'm eerily pale, even when you consider the fact that many red-haired people look drowsy all their lives. Despite my boyish appearance, I feel like a decrepit old man, who's seen it all but is trapped in the body of a young man. From now on I guess it's just a question of killing time until I reach the grave; can anything surprise me anymore?

I place the rose cuttings in the hospital cups on the window-sill and try adjusting the temperature of the radiators a number of times without success. I'm hungry, but since I didn't think of buying anything in the bakery, I can't muster up the energy to go traipsing down and up six floors. Instead I sprawl out on the bed and bury my head under my leather jacket. A moment later, I slip out of my jeans and sweater and crawl under the duvet. I sniff the duvet, but the smell doesn't trigger off any particu-lar associations. I toss and turn under the borrowed sheets. I'm either cold or sweaty; I wouldn't be surprised if I'd developed an infection in my wound and were running a temperature, that's all I need. But I stop myself from sinking into a state of shame-less self-pity. Although I do miss Dad. In fact, I haven't left home yet, and my mind flashes back to my old light blue duvet cover with the pictures of boats on it. I wonder what Dad is eating. He might be boiling the life out of some potatoes at this very moment; then later, when the windows are all fogged up, he'll drop some fish into the pot. Although I don't exactly miss Dad's culinary efforts since Mom died, I somehow always associate Dad's presence with mealtimes. At any rate, I wouldn't say no to some salted cod with spuds and butter. When I was a kid, it was always Dad who used to make the fish palatable for me by taking the bones out of it, putting butter on it, and mashing it into my potatoes. I used to watch him build the yellowish-white hill. He wouldn't spread the food around the plate, because that would make it go cold. It could take quite some time to smoothen all the sides of the volcano, to sharpen the rough and exposed land-scape with Dad's razor-sharp knife. I would only eat two mouth-fuls and then I'd be full and have to go off and do something else. Dad would patiently put me back on the stool and continue spooning fish into me. And where's my brother? Why isn't he at the table with me? Yes, there he is, sitting still opposite me. He eats whatever is put in front of him without any fuss. He doesn't make any remarks, he isn't inquisitive and curious the way I am, he doesn't sink under the table to see what lies below the surface of the world.

—One for Daddy...

Eleven

Although the apartment is on the top floor and the window is closed, the hubbub of city life reaches my bed—beeping cars, shouts, and calls—it all seems so close. Dusk is quick to fall, the sky turns blue at around six, and the city plunges into darkness.

The window overlooks a narrow yard, with a view from the bed of a lit-up neighboring apartment across the way, a kitchen with no curtains, and a dining room, which I guess must be about only twelve feet from my bed. It's like looking at a dollhouse from which the front wall has been removed, offering a sample view of the family life inside. This is the third time in one hour that my female neighbor on the other side of the yard appears in the kitchen dressed in nothing but her underwear. I watch her butter two slices of bread and put cold cuts on them. It's as if the absence of curtains has never even crossed her mind, and at least once or twice, she seems to be looking straight at me. Her panties are a violet red, and she's holding the slice of bread in one hand. Then she briefly steps out of frame, and when she reemerges she's in a dress and there's a man standing with her in the kitchen, taking stuff out of a shopping bag. The girl could be my age, and I immediately substitute myself for the boyfriend. Assuming I could make a miraculously rapid recovery, I would be open to the possibility of getting to know her better if the opportunity were to present itself. Not that I can imagine the opportunity ever arising, though. Nevertheless, I entertain the fantasy of an encounter with her. I might, for example, need an egg—because I do know how to fry an egg—so I might knock on her door. That would mean, of course, having to go down the six floors of my building, out onto the street, passing the shop that sells eggs, and then into her building. And since I don't have a key to my neighbor's front entrance I'd have to find a way of hopping in with one of her unsuspecting neighbors when they were entering and then climb the six flights of stairs to knock on the door to her apartment. I conjure up other ways of approaching her. The simplest thing, of course, would be a chance encounter in the bakery.

—Come on, she'd say, dragging me by the hand across the paved courtyard. Let's go up to my place. Once she strokes my hair in the same way that she stroked her boyfriend's a few moments ago, I'm not sure I'd have anything to say to her. I ponder on whether my experience of six women is a lot or a little for a man of my age. Is it above average, just average, or way below average?

I open the window and the smell of food whets my appetite. I decide to rummage through the kitchen to see if there's anything to eat, and I look into two cupboards. My brief search reveals some rye crackers and packets of asparagus soup. I grab the rhubarb jam from my backpack and eat three crackers with jam while the soup is boiling. I'm taken aback by the quantity of kitchen implements my friend has; she seems to have four of everything. Then I open the cupboard where the crockery is kept and look for some drink receptacle. The cups have floral patterns and gilded rims; I'm scared of dropping her precious china and root through the bottom of the cupboard until I find a plastic cup to drink water from.

What would my home be like?—It takes two to make a home, Mom would say; the only thing I couldn't live without is plants, although I picture myself more out in a garden than standing indoors. I'm not like Dad, who is a born handyman. He doesn't wander into the garage without a tie or a phillips-head screw-driver and reducer close at hand. I'm not one of those DIY guys, like those family men who can do everything: lay pavement, do the electrical wiring, make doors for the kitchen cupboards, build steps, unblock drainpipes, and change windows, or smash a pane of double-glazed glass with a sledgehammer—all those things that a man is supposed to be able to do. If I put my mind to it I could probably do some of those things, if not all of them, but I'd never enjoy them. I could put up some shelves, but putting up shelves could never become a hobby of mine, I wouldn't waste my evenings and weekends on stuff like that. I don't picture myself screwing some shelves together while Dad does the electric wir-ing. My future father-in-law could turn out to be an expert floor layer, so the two fathers-in-law could plan things together, each with his own coffee thermos resting on my shelves. Or the worst thing would be if it were just Dad and me and he'd be teaching me things like I was his apprentice. The more I think about the idea of founding a home, the more I realize I'm not cut out for it. The garden is another story altogether; I could stay in the garden for days and nights on end.

Dad phones me as I'm finishing the asparagus soup. He wants me to confirm that I've eaten. Then he wants to know what was for dinner, so I explain to him that they advise you to eat lightly after an appendix operation and that I had asparagus soup. He tells me that he was invited to Bogga's for lamb soup. Then he asks me about Thórgun and I tell him she's just popped out. He wants to know if I'm recovering and I tell him I'm feeling a lot better. Then he asks if it always gets dark at the same time.

—Yeah, at around six.

—How's the weather? he asks.

—Same as this morning, cloudy and mild, spring weather really.

—What's the electricity like there?

—What do you mean? The lights work, I say.

I know zilch about electricity. Dad tried to teach me how to change a plug on the morning of my ninth birthday, and I remember how stunned he was by my lack of interest. It was as if I were telling him that I had no intention of becoming a man. When he asks me about the electricity, I get the feeling that he's checking my manhood levels.

—I've never liked the darkness, Lobbi lad, says the electrician before wishing me good night.

After saying good-bye to Dad and sending my regards to Jósef, I get into the pajamas they both gave me and lie under the girly duvet. The sleeves and legs are a bit on the short side. Since my operation I've been thinking a lot more about the body, both mine and the bodies of others. When I say the bodies of others I mainly mean the bodies of women, although I notice men's bodies, too. I wonder if my increased awareness of the body might be a side effect of the anesthetic I had four days ago. My tummy is still sore, but nevertheless I feel incredibly lonely under this quilt. The best thing I can come up with is to grope myself, check my body to feel I'm still alive. I start off by feeling its individual elements, as if to persuade myself that they're still a part of me. Although I'm clearly condemned to a period of solitude while I'm recovering from the appendix operation, I can nevertheless tangibly feel the longings of my male body. I can't sleep, and my mind begins to wander. I even wonder if I should have gotten a phone number from the brown-eyed nurse who took care of my rose cuttings and helped me into bed on that first night, the one with the butterfly in her hair. Or the one who helped me into the shower and changed my bandage afterward.

Twelve

The following morning there's a strange cloud in the sky, shaped like a child's bonnet with a frilly rim. Having pulled through my death and resurrection, I'm back on track again, and when I gently press the stitches, the pain is almost completely gone. It automatically makes me look at things differently at the beginning of a new day.

—All it needs is sleep and time, Mom would have said.

I can't say I feel any longing to go home, that there's anything pulling me there. Perhaps it's unusual for a twenty-two-year-old man to be feeling so ecstatic about being alive, but after the misfortunes of the past few days I feel there's cause for celebration. There's no such thing as an ordinary day so long as one is still alive, so long as one's days aren't counted. The plants seem to be doing well on the windowsill; some tiny, white, almost invisible root threads are beginning to form. I decide to get dressed and to go out and buy some food.

The moment I get back in with some bread and salami sausage, the phone rings. It's Dad. He asks me how I am and if I've had any breakfast yet. Then he asks me about Thórgun again and the weather. I tell him about the strange cloud formation, and he tells me they're still being blasted by the harsh northern wind and the grass is withered. Then he says:

—Guess what, your graduation photograph fell off my bedside table and the glass broke.

—There never was any graduation photograph of me.

I didn't have a graduation cap when I graduated. But Mom took a photograph of me in the garden that day. Mom was smart. Then she took a picture of Jósef and me together. He held my hand, as usual; I was a head taller. In the end Jósef took a picture of Mom and me, by the fire lily bed, in which we are both laughing.

I don't know whether he's losing his hearing or whether Dad just chooses to ignore some of the things I say to him.

—I was adjusting it when it fell on the floor. Thröstur at the frame shop is putting it in a new frame, slightly bigger than the one it was in. He agreed with me that it could take a bigger mounting, the white passe-partout will compensate for the absence of the cap.

I no longer have the energy to talk to Dad.

—I chose a mahogany frame.

—Well, I'll have a better chat with you later, Dad.

—Are you happy with mahogany, son?

—Yeah, perfectly happy.

I'm on vacation until my stitches are removed, so I can just lie in bed and read. I read all day. In the evening I dig my gardening book out of my backpack and quickly browse through the first chapter on lawns, the main concern of any gardener, then indoor plants, before I pause on the chapter on trimming trees. From there I move on to an interesting chapter about grafting, which has been difficult to find information on.

In fact, I don't know what awaits me in the garden; there was nothing specific about the job itself in the letter. Although I'd rather devote myself entirely to the roses, I'd also be willing to trim bushes and cut the grass, as long as I get a chance to plant my rose cuttings in the soil. I did find it a bit odd, however, that the monastery I wrote to should ask me about my shoe size.

I'm reading about genetic changes in plants when a key is inserted into the lock and my friend appears in the doorway. I'm under the duvet.

—It's freezing, she says without any formalities, didn't you turn on the heater?

—I couldn't figure out the controls.

—You just have to plug it in and turn it on, she says, taking off a red beret, unwinding the scarf around her neck, and slipping out of her green suede jacket. Then my childhood friend strips down to her panties and pink T-shirt, lifts up the duvet, and asks:

—Any room?

Thirteen

Personally I just don't have the strength at precisely this point in my life, fresh out of the operating room as it were, to go through the steps required to lure a woman into bed. My friend's early return has taken me totally by surprise and thrown me off guard. Had she planned to surprise me? Thorlákur, my ex-friend, would say that women never do anything without a plan.

I ask her why she's come home so soon.

—You said you were only going to be here for a few days and that you were going to buy a secondhand car and head off for some garden, she says, surprised. I expected you'd be gone, she adds.

I watch her almost completely disappear under the duvet and sink into the mattress. She's clearly going to sleep in the bed with me, and since there aren't any other beds in the room you could say we've skipped quite a few steps in the getting-to-know-each-other-a-little-bit-better process.

—But I'm not pushing you to go, she says under the duvet.

—I had to have my appendix out, I say. The stitches will be removed tomorrow.

I tell her about my misfortunes, she shows some interest in the matter, but I pray to god she doesn't ask to see the scar.

—Can I see the scar? She's as excited as a child dying to see a puppy.

Thank god I'm in the pajamas Dad gave me, even though they reflect the taste of a man who'll be eighty in three years' time.

—Nice pajamas.

—Thanks.

I pull back the pajama trousers, just far enough to reveal the scar. Which is quite far down, way below my stomach.

She bursts out laughing. Literally everything about her is new to me and surprises me.

—Didn't you have braces at school?

—Yeah, thirteen to fourteen.

She takes off her glasses and places them on the bedside table. This is her way of saying she won't be reading in bed. I'm still holding my book with a finger stuck inside the chapter on genetic changes in plants.

The thing that throws me the most is seeing my friend without her myopic glasses for the first time, seeing the eyes that have been hidden behind those thick lenses. It's as if they've never been exposed before, like she's premiering her eyes for the first time. She couldn't be more naked without her glasses.

—Are those nearsighted glasses? I ask, shifting the spotlight to the strength and thickness of the lenses in the hope that it will distract my mind from the fact that I'm in bed with my ex–schoolmate who has practically no clothes on. I'm still hoping the glasses can save me and lead us on to the next natural step in our conversation.

—Yeah, minus six on both eyes.

—Have you never considered laser treatment?

—Yes, I've been thinking it over.

I feel a hot shudder moving into my stomach in the cold bedroom and break into a sweat. The pain in my gut has given way to some other kind of feeling.

—Haven't you got some gardening job? she asks. Didn't you say you were going to some rose garden?

—Yeah.

Actually I'm not just heading to any garden, but to a garden that has centuries of history behind it and that's mentioned in all the books about the most famous rose gardens in the world. Some of Father Thomas's letter of reply was a bit hazy and vague, but I was warmly welcomed.

—And weren't you working at sea?

—Yeah.

—What happened to the Latin genius?

—He just evaporated.

She switches subjects.

—Don't you have a child? she asks.

—Yeah, a seventh-month-old girl, I say, but this time resist the temptation to pull out the photograph and show it to her.

—Aren't you a couple, you and the mother?

—No, we just had the kid. It wasn't planned. She was actually a friend of a friend of mine, do you remember Thorlákur? He had a real crush on her for a while, that's how I met her, mainly because he talked about her nonstop, but the feeling wasn't mutual.

—Didn't he go into theology?

—Yeah, so I hear.

—So you're not running away from anything?

She talks like Dad.

—Not at all.

We lie there motionless for a moment, each of us on our own side of the bed. She shuts up. We both shut up.

It was the first winter after Mom died, on my twenty-first birthday, and we'd kind of broken away from the group, Anna and I. It was well into the early hours, and it was snowing. When we stepped into the crunching snow in the garden, the first footprints of the day, we dropped into the snow and made two angels; then I was going to show her the tomato plants. She was studying physiology and was interested in the genetics of plants on this particular night. It might have been five in the morning, and I no longer remember when we got into the greenhouse. There was always light on the plants, and the roses let off a sweet smell. As soon as we staggered into the greenhouse we were hit by hot, humid air, as if we were suddenly on the other side of the planet, inside the thick undergrowth of a one-hundred-square-foot jungle. The gardening tools were kept right by the entrance, and there was also an old sofa bed that I'd moved in there myself when I was studying for my exams, to be able to read close to the plants. And then it was never moved again. Mom also kept an old record player in the greenhouse, and her record collection was a weird concoction from various corners of the globe. Her watering can and pink floral gloves were there, too, as if she'd just popped out a moment. Not that I was thinking of Mom at that moment. We took off our coats, and I chanced upon a record with some kind of climbing plant on the cover, like some ornamental growth from an Indian palace garden, and we danced one close dance. I was used to dancing with my brother Jósef. We were probably talking about botany and, before I knew it, were starting to undress close to the green tomatoes. Most of the rest is blurred in my memory. For a moment, though, I thought I saw something glowing in the night, so strangely close, like a light beaming through the falling snow. For an instant, the greenhouse was filled with a blinding brightness, and the light pierced through the plants projecting petal patterns against my friend's body. I caressed the rose petals on her stomach, and at the same moment we both clearly felt a whirlwind, like the sound of a fan that someone had just switched on. It wasn't until much later that I remembered the detail of the whirlwind and started to think about that glow in the darkness as if it hadn't been an altogether natural phenomenon. Immediately after it, we heard the voice of a man outside the greenhouse, standing beside the mound of snow. As I suspected, it was the neighbor holding a flashlight, calling his dog. When daylight broke there were two angels printed in the snow, linked together at the hands, like part of a chain of paper dolls. If Mom had been alive she would have stared at me over the breakfast table with a mysterious knowing air. And because I had no appetite for my breakfast, she was bound to have said that I was getting too skinny.

—Or are you still growing? she'd ask, gazing up at her lanky son with a smile. She was always worried about the three men in her life wasting away and that I in particular didn't eat enough. Then I didn't hear from the expectant mother of my child for another two months. It was just around the New Year that she phoned to ask if we could meet in a café.

Fourteen

I can't really say that I'm in a decent enough physical state to be able to sleep with anyone at the moment. To be honest, I'd probably prefer the gardening book to take precedence over the girl right now. But can I say no, I'm sorry? Wouldn't that offend her and make what follows pretty awkward?

—Did you bring plants? she asks pointing at the rose cuttings in the hospital cups on the windowsill.

—Yeah, those are rose cuttings from the greenhouse back home, I say. I'm taking them to the garden.

—Does it have a special name, the rose?

—Yeah, eight-petaled rose.

—Where does this interest in plants come from? she asks.

—I was more or less brought up in a greenhouse, I feel good in flower beds.

I imagine her interest in gardening is limited and realize that, since I can't really think of anything else to talk about, I might be forced to take our communication to another level, beyond words. I'm facing two options here: to do or not to do. The question is, when exactly does the decision time run out? In five minutes, ten minutes, or has it maybe already expired? I take off my watch and stretch over her to put it on the bedside table. My confirmation mate is awake and staring at me with big eyes; it's difficult to actually figure out what's going through her mind. Not that it makes much difference, my mind is just as foggy and unclear.

❋

Fifteen

Then there's also the fact that one can't always remember every-thing one does, so that when one wakes up and sees a head of curly hazel hair on the other side of the bed, one has to start off by checking who's under the quilt. Not that I'd like to give the impression that I often get into the situation of not remembering exactly who is lying under the covers with me. In the case of my childhood friend, however, my recollection of yesterday evening and night are quite clear. She is still asleep, but I manage to climb over her and slip out of the bed without waking her. I feel dizzy when I stand up but manage to swiftly get into my trousers. Then I go down to the bakery to buy some breakfast for Thórgun. I also feel the need to thank her, so I buy some flowers, a pink potted plant. After that I really need to get going.

She's already up by the time I get back and sticks her head out of the kitchen. She's in a semi-long patterned skirt garment over her blue jeans and wearing a coat, as if she's about to leave at that very moment. She's put her glasses back on so I feel secure again. I have to admit I was a bit surprised she was about to leave without saying good-bye. I hand her the bag from the bakery and the potted plant. It's a dahlia.

—I got something to eat with the coffee, I say.

—Thanks, she says, sniffing the plant.

It's almost odorless; maybe I should have chosen something with a stronger scent.

—It should be OK on its own for a few days, I say, while you're digging up graveyards.

—How's your wound? she asks.

—Much better, almost normal again, I say. I speak the truth, although I still have to be careful when I'm zipping up my fly.

My schoolmate says she has to dash. Still, she peeks into the bakery bag and chooses some kind of glazed doughnut, although she says she doesn't have time for breakfast.

—I have a class to get to, she says, still holding the pot, so I'll just say bon voyage and all the best on your journey to the promised garden with your eight-petaled roses.

—Thanks a lot for putting me up, I say. I take the potted plant from her and place it on the kitchen table. Then I put my arms around her and pat her once or twice down the back. Finally I adjust her scarf, wrapping it better around her neck.

—Thanks again, I repeat.

—I don't want to hold you up, she says, quickly getting her things together, shoving books into her bag, and fetching something from the bathroom. Then she gives me a hasty kiss and slowly moves along the wall toward the door. She pauses in front of the mirror a moment to check her reflection and adjust the clasp in her thick, curly hair. This means she's about to leave but has still left something unsaid. She lingers in the doorway holding the glazed doughnut she's going to eat on her way to the archaeological museum.

—Maybe you're not particularly into women?

The question completely throws me. How should I answer? Should I say yes I am, but not into every woman on the planet? Would my friend be offended by that? Or should I just say things as they are? That up until this morning I just haven't accumulated enough experience to pass any verdicts on that? Or should I use the state of my body to justify myself and once more show her the black stitches protruding from my groin. That way I could say:

—Yeah, but not with the stitches.

—Don't take it personally, my confirmation sister says, with one foot through the door. The archaeology student is wearing high leather boots with heels.

I glance at the alarm clock on the bedside table as I get my stuff together and make the bed: it takes me about four minutes.

Sixteen

It doesn't take me long to find the right car: a nine-year-old lemon yellow Opel Lasta 37 awaits me on the street. It's got a radio and seems to be in reasonably good shape, clean both outside and inside. It's been vacuum cleaned and the ashtrays have been emptied. It actually had a hell of a lot of mileage on it, ninety-six thousand miles, but it was at a bargain price, a real giveaway as Dad would say. I pay for the car, counting the notes on the counter. The salesman gawks at me, then stamps the receipt and scribbles his initials under it. Once the stitches have been removed at the hospital, I can set off on my journey. First, though, I stop off at a flower market in the city outskirts to buy some soil for the rose cuttings. I'm unable to resist the impulse to buy an additional two slightly bigger potted rose plants; then I loosely press the soil around the very fine white roots with my fingers and carefully place the plants in the trunk. I'm facing the sun to begin with, things couldn't be simpler. Even if I might be still searching for myself, at least I know where I'm headed.

At the first gas station I buy some bottles of water for the plants, a map to follow, a sandwich to have for lunch, and a notebook to keep a record of numerical data: mileage and expenses. As I'm about to pay and the woman at the register has already, in fact, added everything up, I bend over a packet of condoms stacked right up against the cash register and place it on the map. I won't allow the unexpected to catch me unawares when providence and opportunity knock on my door just like on anyone else's. There are ten condoms in the box; they could last me several days or several years.

I call Dad from a phone booth when I come out of the gas station, just to tell him my stitches have been removed and that I'm on the road.

—You won't be driving down any fast motorways, now, Lobbi.

—No, I'll be taking the country roads just like I said.

—Foreigners don't drive under seventy-five, he says. Not that we're any great example either. You just have to open the paper here. They caught some lad your age doing eight-five miles an hour on the gravel road through the summerhouse area last weekend. He was in a company car with an ad for moss killer, which everyone noticed when he darted up the road. They caught him at the next road café, he'd just ordered French fries, no license.

—Don't worry, the car I bought doesn't do more than forty-five miles an hour, I say, although strictly speaking I'm outside Dad's jurisdiction here.

—There are lots of temptations for men abroad, Lobbi, and many a young lad has been led into them.

Then he tells me that Jósef is coming for dinner and that he was thinking of inviting Bogga as well because she invited him for the lamb soup the other day.

The problem is he can't decipher Mom's recipes.

—They're on loose notes, the writing isn't always legible, and she doesn't seem to mention portions or ratios. There are no numbers on the sheets.

—What were you thinking of cooking?

—Halibut soup.

—I seem to remember that halibut soup is quite difficult to make.

—I've bought the halibut. Question is when do the prunes come into it and whether they should be left soaked in water from the morning, like she used to do when she was making her prune pudding.

—I don't think she soaked the prunes in water in the morning when she was making halibut soup.

That's my recollection, too.

—Right then, Dad, I'll call you sometime along the road.

—You take it easy now, Lobbi.

I unfold the map over the lemon-yellow hood and plot my route. I don't know this territory, but look at the place names, road numbers, and distances. I see that if I take the old pilgrim's route, which crosses three borders, I'm bound to end up taking unforeseen detours and prolonging my journey. But, on the other hand, that would give me a chance to familiarize myself with the vegetation and chat with some of the natives. Since I'm going to have to frequently ask for directions, I'll be meeting people and practicing the local language and eating in homey restaurants. I randomly plant my index on the map and decide that's where I'll stay tonight, somewhere around there, give or take a centimeter or two. Which corresponds to give-or-take one hundred twenty-five miles in the real world. Great wars had been waged for far less, even just for a few millimeters here and there. I drag my index finger all along the route to my destination, which is way out on the very edge of the map, at the very bottom of the hood. The place isn't specifically marked on the map, but I think the pilgrim's route ends close by. I give myself five days to reach my destination, the rose garden.

✳

Seventeen

With both hands on the wheel, I watch the pilgrim's way unwind, bend after bend, as I drive through the forest with trees on all sides. I'm facing the sun until noon, but then it shifts between mirrors as the day passes.

It suits me fine to be on my own, although it might have been easier if I'd had a copilot with me to read the map and avoid wrong turns. Instead every now and then I turn on the turn signal and pull to the side of the road in this dark green forest, turn off the engine, peer over the map, and then water the plants in the trunk while I'm at it. Of course, you have to keep your eyes peeled for wild deer or boar and other small creatures on this road. I try to remember what kind of animals I might expect to find. I can almost hear Dad's voice beside me:

—Woods can be dodgy places, they've got bears and wolves in them and wicked people, too. Some crime is probably being committed right now in the thick of the woods just a few yards away, and it'll probably be reported in the local press tomorrow. And young girls posing as hitchhikers could easily be the bait used by criminal gangs. Once they've stopped a car the gang pops up from the behind the bushes.

Dad's worries can be smothering; unlike him, I trust people. I suddenly look to my side; no, Mom isn't there.

I feel Mom is beginning to fade; I'm so scared that soon I won't be able to conjure it all up again. I therefore replay our final conversation in my mind when she called me from the car wreckage, and I dwell on every conceivable detail. Mom had intended to phone Dad but I answered. He'd given her the mobile phone shortly before it happened, but I didn't realize she actually used it or carried it around with her. In order for her to continue to exist I constantly have to discover new things about her; with each flashback I collect new information about things I didn't know before.

Dad hadn't said bye to her any differently that morning, but he found it difficult to forgive me for having answered the phone and even more difficult to forgive himself for not being at home. He wanted to be the one to own Mom's last words, for her not to leave without delivering her last words to him.

—She needed me and I was out in a store buying an extension, he said.

He was so terribly disappointed that Mom died before he did, sixteen years younger, she was, as he constantly repeated, only fifty-nine. He'd imagined things so differently.

She says she's had a little mishap and that the "road crew" have come to help her, strong fellows—and that I needn't worry, she was in good hands, they were working fast, the boys, and on top of things.

—Did you burst a tire, Mom?

—I must have, she says in a calm and collected voice. I could well believe I burst a tire. The car seemed to go a bit wobbly.

There might have been a slight tremor in her voice, but she told me not to worry about her twice, she'd just had a slight mishap—that was exactly how she put it—a slight mishap, and out of sheer clumsiness. She'd call me again once they'd got the car back up on the road again, the road crew, as she called them, as if she were some rally driver and they were four assistants.

—Did you go off the road?

—You better take care of the dinner for yourself and your father if I'm not back on time; you can heat up the fish balls from yesterday, it'll be a while yet.

Then she takes a brief pause before starting on her description of the autumn color paradise she's in. I'm totally puzzled by the sunlight she talked about. It was raining all over the country, and according to the police's report, it was precisely the wetness of the road that had caused the accident. It was all wet, the asphalt was wet, the fields were wet, the lava field was wet, and yet she described the stunning shades of the landscape, how the sun gilded the moss out in the middle of the black lava field. She spoke about this beautiful light, she spoke about the light, yeah, about the light.

—Are you out in the lava field, Mom? Are you hurt at all, Mom?

—I probably need to get new frames for my glasses.

I know the phone call is coming to an end now, but to prolong the duration of the memory, to postpone Mom's farewell in my mind, to keep her with me for longer, I embellish the script of the flashback with elements that I didn't get to say on the spur of the moment.

—But, Mom, but, Mom, I was just wondering if we should maybe try to move your eight-petaled roses out of the greenhouse into the garden, out into the flower bed, and see if they survive the winter.

Or I could ask something that would take her longer to explain:

—How do you make your curry sauce, Mom? And cocoa soup, Mom, and halibut soup?

Then I thought I heard her say, but I'm not sure about this, that I should be tolerant of Dad even though he was a bit old-fashioned and eccentric in his ways. And continue to be good to my brother Jósef.

—Be good to your dad. And don't forget your brother Jósef. You held his hand when you were still in the carriage—might she have said that?

Then I hear a faint shuddering breath, like the beginning of pneumonia; Mom has stopped talking.

The conversation is over, but I hear a background murmur of male voices.

—Is the phone still on? someone asks.

—She's gone, it's over, another voice can be heard saying.

Then someone picks up the phone.

—Hello, is there anyone there? they ask.

I say nothing.

—He's hung up, the voice says at the end of the line.

—The tow truck is here, another voice can be heard saying.

—We couldn't reach her properly with the shears while she was still alive and really couldn't do much for her, says one of the ambulance men who fully understands that I want to ask questions. But we saw that she was talking on the phone, which was incredible, considering how badly hurt the woman was; she must have been steadily swallowing blood. There was never any hope, no hope of her ever surviving this while she waited to be cut out of the wreckage.

Her clothes and glasses were returned to us in a bag, along with her berry-picking rake and various other objects that she had with her in the car. Her glasses were covered in blood with both lenses cracked, one arm twisted back ninety degrees.

Dad and I took care of the flowers on the coffin. I wanted to have wildflowers, meadowsweet, chervil, wood cranesbill, buttercups, and lady's mantle, but Dad wanted something more solemn, bought in a shop, imported roses. In the end, though, he gave in and left the floral arrangements to his son.

Eighteen

I'm still in the forest, which seems endless and spans the entire spectrum of green. This gives me the seclusion I need to sort out my thoughts, as Dad would put it, not that I expect to have reached any concrete conclusions by the end of these one thousand twenty-seven miles. Most of my current thoughts—apart from sticking to the right side of the road—are on last night. What still bugs me and throws me and dominates all my thoughts for the first one hundred miles is the radical transformation of my childhood friend, to see her as a new person without glasses and with a woman's body. I could actually ask myself the same question she asked me: whether I'm not particularly into women. I can easily put up with a woman for half a night, but I'm not sure I can protect one against anything she might be afraid of. Girls generally have a lot more to say than I have; they tell you stuff, like about their relationship with their granddad they grew up with, and how he taught them chess and took them to concerts before he got cancer of the bladder. Sometimes they tell you something sad that's happened to the family, maybe even last century, if there haven't been any other tragedies in recent years, other than maybe Granddad dying and then sometimes Granny dying shortly after that. Women have very long memories and are sensitive to the bizarre events that have colored their family histories over the past two hundred years. Then they even try to link me to their family trees. I find it difficult to open myself up like that to other people, although I'm perfectly willing to sleep with a girl.

I get the feeling there might be an extra sound coming from the car. If any mechanical problem were to come up, I wouldn't have the required macho-ness to fix it. I'm just not that kind of guy. I could change a tire, but not a spark plug or a fan belt. I haven't the faintest interest in engines. No one is expecting me for dinner, but I have to find some lodging for myself, and I better hurry before there's total darkness and it's impossible to find my way. Even though dark forests can give you the creeps, I reassure myself that there's nothing to fear, because I know that somewhere within the darkness there's some human settlement, some invisible village with a church and post office by a small paved square. I'm hungry, and beside the church there will probably be a restaurant with white lace curtains. Then, beside the restaurant, there might be a guesthouse. Because these are all roads that have been traveled on for thousands of years. Of course, it's a completely different experience to take the pilgrim's route instead of driving on brand-new asphalt roads that have been laid over rough, barren black lava.

I scan the horizon for a landmark, such as a church. There's obviously a lot going on in the sky, a half-moon and constellations glistening like swarms of silver butterflies. I don't notice the church until it suddenly pops up in my rearview mirror; I've missed the turn and have to reverse to find the side road through the forest. There isn't a soul in sight, and I certainly wouldn't want to be stranded here. Driving a short distance farther, however, I find a sign for a restaurant with an arrow pointing even deeper into the woods, with the distance written beside it: one mile. I follow the sign and drive down a faint trail through the dark forest. One side road leads into another; the signs are homemade, as if children had made them in some treasure hunt game. Although I only have a very basic grasp of the language, I notice there's a letter missing in one word. I first spot the steeple of the church; then I make out a track, until the church shrinks and grows more distant and starts to look like a LEGO model in my rearview mirror. I'm in the middle of the woods, literally surrounded by trees on every side, and I haven't the faintest idea of where I am. Can a person who has been brought up in the heart of a thick dark forest, where one has to beat a path through multiple layers of trees just to take a letter to the post office, have any conception of what it's like to spend one's entire childhood waiting for a single tree to grow?

Nineteen

Just when I think I have completely lost my bearings, an inn appears at the end of the side road. As expected, there are white lace curtains in the windows. There's one car in the driveway. I walk past the front side of the house until I reach the kitchen. The skinned furs of forest animals adorn the walls in a row: hares, rabbits, and wild boar. The owner comes out the door to greet me and ushers me into a small dining room with a few tables. There are more furs on the walls and stuffed stag heads, along with a collection of guns. I'm clearly the only guest. The place gives off a pleasant odor of cleanliness and food. There are white tablecloths on the table and linen napkins, three glasses per plate, and three sets of knives and forks of different sizes.

I'm none the wiser after reading the menu, which the man tries to talk me through over my shoulder, but I can't follow the thread.

—One moment, he says, to prevent me from immediately turning around, and he fetches a woman from the kitchen in a lily-white apron whom I imagine he must have lived with for several decades because he doesn't even need to explain the problem to her. The woman presents me with my options:

—Would you like this or would you prefer this? asks the woman.

I just nod. The woman suddenly bursts out laughing.

—Which do you want? she asks.

This is the worst question she could have asked me, and it throws me into a panic. I don't know what I want; there's still so much I've yet to try and understand.

—That's the problem, I say to the woman, I don't know what I want.

I imagine you can't really sink much lower than this on the estimation scale of a restaurant in a forest, not even to know what you want to eat. The woman nods, full of understanding.

—I'll just take what you recommend, I say to settle the matter. The woman seems pleased; this isn't the first time I've asked a woman to make decisions for me.

—Trust me, she says in a manner that is both mysterious and trustworthy, you won't be disappointed.

A short while later, as I sit alone in the room under the reindeer's head, the woman returns with a dish and bottle of wine. It turns out to be the first of many dishes. She pours the wine into one of the glasses.

—I took the liberty of choosing the wine as well, she says, enjoy your meal. She recoils slightly and observes my reactions.

—How do you like it? she asks.

—Very good, I say, tasting a lukewarm pâté in a wild mushroom sauce.

—I thought as much.

She brings over a photograph of a porcupine to show me the source of the pâté. The porcupine pâté is followed by at least another three starters, pâté upon pâté, wild boar pâté, duck pâté, and goose pâté; then after that, three of the forest restaurant's specialties: breast of fallow deer, moose fillets, shoulder of venison, one meat dish after another. According to the collection of photographs that the woman presents with each dish, everything that's brought to me, literally everything comes from the forest. These are the creatures that I've been scared of running over all day, now cooked. There isn't much along the lines of vegetables; instead there are sauces and bread. The woman insists on me drinking a glass of wine with each dish. The couple are very soft spoken and ask me a number of questions that I try to answer as much as my knowledge of the language will allow. Every time a new dish is carried in I think, that's it, the meal's over. The man asks where I'm headed and I tell him. At various intervals a girl around my age wanders into the room. She comes and goes and seems to acknowledge me; I notice she's wearing a dotted skirt. I get the feeling that the whole family is observing me, that there's some purpose behind all this.

But I can't deny that the food is excellent and the bill ludicrously low. Since I've knocked back too many glasses to be able to carry on with my journey, I ask the woman about accommodation in the forest. It seems to be on the couple's top floor, so I fetch my backpack and then my plants from the car. As the family watches me from the stairs, the man asks me if I'm a gardener, and I say you could say that. The woman tells me I can pay for the dinner tomorrow, and after drinking a cranberry liqueur on the house, I water the plants one last time, brush my teeth, undress, and dive under the lily-white sheets.

Twenty

I'm still full when I come down the following morning: a breakfast table has nonetheless been set for me under the stag's head,
with some home-baked bread in a basket and three types of some
kind of sweet pastry. There are also some homemade jams on
the table, made with forest berries, the woman explains to me,
two boiled eggs, several slices of meat, and the leftovers of the
porcupine pâté from the night before, as far as I can make out.
Once I'm seated, the woman approaches with fruit juice, coffee,
and hot milk and asks if I might like a cup of hot chocolate after
my coffee. The girl is sitting at a table at the opposite end of the
room by the rifle collection and is drinking hot chocolate from
a bowl. She's wearing a red hairband, but I can't see if she's still
wearing her spotted skirt. There are no other breakfast guests in
the room.

Once I've loaded my stuff into the car, I go back in to pay
for last night's feast, the accommodation, and the breakfast. The
total on the bill hasn't changed since last night, and I don't see
any extra charge for the room. If I didn't have any important
tasks to attend to, I could live a good life here and spend long
hours in the forest on just a few months of my sailor's wages.
When I've finished settling the bill and have just started the Opel
and am about to turn it around in the cul-de-sac, I see the owner
of the restaurant coming down the steps and waving at me. I
wind the window down.

—The thing is, he says, I have someone here who needs a lift,
as it were.

The request catches me off guard, and my mastery of the language is too poor to enable me to immediately find the right words to string a sentence together that politely says no and then apologize for and explain the reason for the no. It would have been too humiliating to pull out a dictionary.

—Well, the person is my daughter. She's studying drama in a town just a stone's throw away from here and was just home for the weekend. I can't drive her there myself; we're expecting a guest this afternoon.

—How far is it from here?

—Two hundred and thirteen miles altogether, says the father, who is used to shuttling her.

He's had enough time to observe me wrestling with the culinary specialties of the house and now deems me trustworthy enough to drive his daughter to her drama course. I probably look innocent enough with my ginger hair and pure boyish looks—those are the words Mom would have used. You can't judge a book by its cover, though; my obsessive thoughts about the body remain invisible to the world. Two hundred and thirteen miles is a lot of time to be spending with an unknown drama student. But the family has meticulously planned the move, leaving me with no leeway to reject my traveling companion. While I'm still dumbstruck and trying to formulate a grammatically correct reply in my mind, the girl comes running out of the building with fluttering hair, and she has switched her red hairband with a black one. She's wearing a short violet coat with a thick belt around her waist and carrying a bag, so she's ready to go. On her way to the car, she somehow weaves her hair into a bun and ties it with an elastic. Then she kisses her father on both cheeks and they exchange a few words. I don't know what they're talking about, but the father vanishes into the house and she tells me to wait, signaling that there's more to come. When he swiftly returns, he's holding a box in his arms that looks quite heavy and signals me with his head to open the trunk so that he can fit it in there.

—For you, the daughter interprets.

He wants to show me the contents of the box first so he comes right up to me with it, tipping it slightly. I count twelve bottles of red wine.

—Our own production, says the girl.

The labels on the bottles carry a fine ink drawing of the parish church with the master's family name under it. This is probably the wine I drank one or two bottles of last night.

—It's the least I can do for the lift, says the father.

The favor for the daughter is valued at twelve bottles. He wants to put his wine into the car himself, but once I've made it clear to him that there's no room in the trunk because of the plants and he has scanned the car, he decides to place the box on the floor in the back. Then he appears once more on the driver's side and gently knocks on the glass with two fingers. I wind down the window again, and he stretches his arm into the car with something clasped in the palm of his hand that he squeezes into mine. Cash.

—The food and the lodging is on the house, and the rest is for the gas, he says with a chirpy air. I'll just say safe journey then.

Some legs wriggle into the car and the daughter blows some more kisses to her father, having just said good-bye to her mother on the steps. Then they wave to each other and I see the man shrinking in the rearview mirror as I drive down the side road. The daughter kneels on the passenger seat with her back to the windshield and her hip up against my shoulder until her father fades from view. I instantly regret having agreed to take her with me in my moment of weakness.

—Put your belt on, I say, pointing at the seat belt and illus-
trating my simple sentence with an appropriate gesture. She
looks at me with a reluctant air, but then breaks into a beaming
smile, puts her leg down, and clicks on the seat belt. Now that I
get a chance to take a better look at the girl I can see she really
looks like a budding movie star.

—Just as you desire.

Just as you desire. I mull that line over in my head, wondering if there might be any hidden meaning in that "just as you
desire." Wondering if I can also apply that "just as you desire" to
other things and what things those might be. And if I did apply
it to other things would she then accept my desire? When I'm
back on the pilgrim's road I, nonetheless, take my right hand
off the steering wheel to shake her hand and formally introduce
myself.

—Arnljótur Thórir.

She smiles at me.

This dainty actress's handshake is tight and firm. Before I
manage to reach any conclusion, I wonder, as I shake her hand,
whether I'm likely to sleep with her at any point over the next two
hundred and thirteen miles.

I haven't been driving for long along the highway when
she bends over and pulls a red box out of her drama student
bag, not unlike a kid's school lunchbox. She opens it, takes out
a sandwich, wraps it in a white napkin, and hands it to me.
Then she takes out another one for herself, also wraps a napkin around it, and sinks back into her seat. Looking into the
sandwich in my hand, I see it contains slices of meat, and this
less than half an hour after I finished my three-course breakfast, and half a day since I completed the biggest meal I've ever
eaten.

Then my twig-skinny co-passenger pulls a pile of papers out of her bag, tucks her legs under her on the front seat, and I see her memorizing a script. She's silent for the first fifteen miles as she learns her part.

Twenty-one

It's not that having another person sitting in the passenger seat beside me bothers me in itself, so long as she remains silent and just reads her words, and sits reasonably still. In any case, it's clear that I'm going to be sitting beside this actress for the next six hours. I peep at her; right above her long, thick eyelashes there is a very fine black streak of eyeliner. In fact, she reminds me of a familiar and very famous film star that I saw in a movie once.

After a while, the actress rolls up the script, points it at me, and kicks off the conversation by asking me where I'm from.

So I tell her.

—Are you really? she exclaims, shifting position on the seat by placing her right foot on the floor, dragging her left leg under her, and slipping the seat belt under her armpit so that she can face me better as she continues the conversation.

—What's it like there?

—There isn't an awful lot to say about the place; there aren't many things you can grow there.

I'm not sure I have much to add to that. She only speaks her language, which I've actually studied at school, although I've never had to express myself in long sentences with an actual native before.

—Tell me something about it.

—Moss.

—Cute.

As soon as I spurt out the word *moss*, I know I've gotten myself into a jam. Moss is such a nonstarter and impossible to develop into a topic for discussion. At most, I could list off the different types of moss, but that's not much of a conversation.

—What's moss?

If I only had the vocabulary, I would want to tell this budding movie star that moss is a lichen, and time-consuming to walk over. It's all right for the first ten steps, but if you're going to cross a vast, moss-carpeted lava field, it's like walking across a trampoline all day; it can be really tiring on your hamstrings to be sinking into moss for four hours in a row. It can take more out of you than climbing a high mountain. If you rip up moss, you leave a scar in the earth and soil dust gets blown into your eyes. I'd really like to be able to tell her something unusual that no one has ever told her before, but my limited grasp of the language cramps my style. If I were to mention the different shades of moss and the smell it gives off after a shower of rain, I'd be entering the domain of feelings, like a man on the point of proposing to her. I therefore give nothing away to her and say no more than I can grammatically handle:

—A plant that's like a trampoline.

—Weird, she says. She doesn't give in—Tell me more.

—Tussocks.

I'm surprised at how well I'm doing at finding words, at my ability to express myself in an alien language, but at least I'm myself when I talk about plants.

—What's a tussock?

It's not easy to explain how a tussock is formed, to express the repeated temperature changes of the earth and how they alternate between frost and thaw. I have to think of every single word I'm saying; nothing comes automatically.

—It's difficult to put up a tent on tussocks.

Then I switch topics.

—Swamps.

On the point of swamps, Mom told me more than once the story of one of Granddad's favorite horses, which sank under him in a swamp and then popped up again as a skeleton several springs later. I've seen photographs of Granddad on that horse, and although I'm no expert, that favorite horse of his looks pretty much like all his other horses to me, with rather short legs, even when you take into consideration the fact that my granddad and namesake, Arnljótur Thórir, was a tall man.

After swamps, I rattle off the names of other types of vegetation without any further explanations, which the actress seems to accept. The Latin names of the plants help me through the most difficult parts of the conversation, and she nods, so I manage to give her an overview of the main features of the local vegetation. I'm on home ground now, with the situation well in hand, and I realize that I've tapped conversation material for the next thirty to forty miles: a revision of the Latin names of plants. I mention the clusters of yellow grass, blueberry heaths, and moss campion.

—Then there's geraniums, meadowsweet, mountain avens, sheep sorrel, prickly rose, burnet rose, and lady's mantle, I say.

—Hang on, lady's what? What lady?

I don't have to go into the botany in any depth, but just rattle off the different species of plants that spring to mind, which is more than enough for my traveling companion to ponder on, as I give her the full lowdown on my roots.

—Angelica, I say. It can reach human height.

—Can it really? she says.

—The grass.

—Grass?

—Yeah, the grass is green all summer, shimmering green, incredibly green.

I stroll across the moor in my mind and through the lush grass until I finally find it, a cluster of lady's mantle. I glance at the clock and see that it's taken me about a quarter of an hour to present the vegetation. My limited knowledge of the grammar soon leads me down a blind alley, preventing me from developing my ideas any further. I end my overview on dwarf fireweed.

—Pink dwarf weed grows on black-sand beaches, in isolated spots here and there.

I think it's important that a person who is brought up in the middle of a forest should understand this, that a flower can grow in isolation, all on its own out of black sand and sometimes in a canyon, too. The moment I mention dwarf fireweed I find myself getting a bit sensitive about it.

—Do you pick flowers there, the fireweed?

—No, it's put so much effort into growing all by itself, sometimes with only just one or two flowers in a whole stretch of sand.

I'm practicing the language, just nouns and verbs, and then I choose a preposition to wrap around the plants and give my traveling companion some idea of the environments they live in. I shift from the canyon down to the sea and enlarge the shore. I think it's equally important that this foreign lass—I say "lass" just like my old man does—to picture the deserted wide expanse of the beach, with no footprints, and then nothing but endless ocean and maybe some breaking waves foaming out in the sea and finally the endless sky above. I say "endless" twice because I want to convey what it's like to follow no other man's footsteps on the black beach. I omit the screeching seagulls, though; they disturb the silence of the image. What's the word for "endless"? If I could say "endless" I could elevate our conversation to a metaphysical level. The actress urges me on:

—Timeless?

—No, not exactly.

—Immortal?

—Yeah, that's closer, I say, immortal.

—Cute, she says.

It occurs to me that I could also try to describe the sound of crunching virgin snow, the first steps of the day.

—In a way it's similar to the black-sand beach, I say, it's all about footprints.

The actress nods.

I think it's absolutely incredible the lengths to which women will go to give me their undivided attention and attempt to grasp what I'm saying. Sometimes uncritically even, it seems. Not that this girl looks in any way desperate; on the contrary. I wouldn't be surprised if I have yet to see her treading the red carpets of film festivals.

Twenty-two

Then I can't be bothered to talk about the vegetation anymore. I just want to shut up for the next hundred miles. I quickly try to calculate how many more miles I'll have to share with my traveling companion. As soon as I stop thinking about grammar I start thinking about the body again. My linguistic limitations could take our relationship straight to another level, to the wordless communication of body language.

Anyway, I have to check on my plants, so I turn on the blinker, pull up on the side of the road, and kill the engine. She unclips her seat belt as well and prepares to follow me to the trunk to investigate. When she opens the door on the passenger side and I simultaneously open the door on mine, she somehow manages to lose her grip on the script, and white sheets scatter in all directions. She doesn't go chasing after them into the thicket, but manages to catch them in a sequence of agile and collected moves, moving as swiftly as possible, though, like a wild animal poised for attack, ready to pin down its prey with its high-heeled paws as soon as it moves. I hand her some sheets as a token gesture, but once I see that she has the situation well in hand, I let her chase after the rest of *A Doll's House* herself and open the trunk instead.

—Hey, what are you doing with these plants? she asks—Is that marijuana? She looks at me with suspicion as I water the plants with the bottles.

—No, these are roses, rose cuttings from home and two extra ones for safety here.

The actress bursts out laughing.

—Have you got a girlfriend? she bluntly asks when we're sitting back in the car again.

—No, but I have a child.

This is the third time on this trip that I feel a compulsion to talk about my daughter.

She shifts excitedly in her seat and seems to have removed her seat belt.

—Put your belt on, I say.

—Are you joking?

—There are all kinds of creatures roaming around here. I point at a sign with a reindeer.

—About the child?

—No, I'm not joking. A girl, about seven months old, I add.

—Are you divorced?

—Her mother isn't my ex-wife, just the mother of my child. There's a big difference.

—Those things normally go together.

—Not where I come from.

—How long were you together?

—Half a night, I say. She's the one who left, I say, not to give the impression that I'd kicked her out. She's the one who got dressed and left.

My traveling companion looks at me, intrigued.

—There's a picture of my daughter in my backpack, I say pointing at the back. She quickly loosens her belt, turns on the light, and then squeezes herself between the seats to rummage through my stuff. Her ass is pretty much against my shoulder while she digs into the top pocket of my backpack.

—In the wallet?

—In the passport.

—Is that your ex-girlfriend?

—No, that's Mom.

I'd forgotten about the photograph of Mom.

In the picture Mom is standing against the lily-blue wall of the house with fire lilies reaching up to her waist. I'm the person who is with her in the picture, but strange as it may sound, it was my brother Jósef who took the picture. I had both set the focus and set my brother, by drawing a line in the soil where he was supposed to stand with his toes, and I'd shown him twice how the press the shutter release. It worked on the fourth attempt, and Mom and I burst out laughing. I'm a head higher than she is and have my arm around her shoulder. She's wearing a violet sweater and a skirt and boots: Mom never wore trousers in the greenhouse or garden.

But she often wore strong colors, which sometimes had peculiar patterns, and she was fond of all kinds of materials, which she liked to stroke and sometimes invited me to touch, to feel the difference between, say, Dralon and chiffon. She sometimes came home with some material and sat at the sewing machine. Next day she'd be sitting at the kitchen table in a new blouse. Strange, that detail about the shoulders, I don't remember holding her like that. She looks happy.

My traveling companion turns again.

—I found it.

She's holding my passport, which contains all my main details, and the photographs of Mom and my daughter. I quickly glance at the picture she's holding up in the air and then at the road again.

—That's her, that's Flóra Sól in the picture. My headlights beam straight into a rabbit's red eyes. It wouldn't be much fun to have scraps of meat stuck in the treads of my tires the next time I pull into a gas station. I should ask if this forest will ever come to an end.

—Cute, she says a moment later, examining the photograph and holding it up to the light. Not very like you, though.

—I don't have a copy of the DNA test on me. I manage to make myself understood; I manage to crack a joke.

She laughs.

—Seven months, you say? She doesn't have a lot of hair for a girl, practically bald.

I correct her.

—She's about seven months, I say. It's tiring to have to explain the same things to everyone, the thing about the hair. The picture is a month old; she was only six months when that was taken. It's not immediately visible, the hair, when it's that blond.

I make one final attempt at explaining to this unfortunate person that blond children generally don't have much hair in the first year. Why was I such an ass to bring the child up? What possessed me to show her the photograph?

—Give it to me, I say, removing one hand from the wheel to take the picture, which she hands back to me without protest.

I quickly glance at my daughter, smiling broadly with her two lower gum teeth, before shoving the photograph into the breast pocket of my shirt under my sweater. There's nothing in that child that indicates that she's the fruit of a half-night stand. Even though my daughter hasn't occupied much space in my life up until now, I expect I'll be giving her more thought in the future. I just have to get used to her. A man is bound to feel some fondness for his own child; he'd be a poor sod if he didn't.

—Weren't you surprised when you discovered that you were expecting a child with a woman you didn't know?

—Yeah, a bit, I say, but then decide to drop the subject with her.

Twenty-three

The expectant mother of my child phoned me around New Year and asked me if I could meet her in a café. When I was seated she told me straight out that she was pregnant.

—We're expecting a child next summer.

I was totally flabbergasted, but couldn't think of anything better to do than to call the waiter over and order a glass of milk. She had a hot chocolate. For a brief moment I stared at the crumbs on the tabletop; they hadn't wiped the table after the last customer.

—Do you normally drink milk? she asked.

—No, actually, I don't.

She laughed. I laughed, too. I was relieved she was laughing. Now, as I try to recall it, what I mainly remember is her profile as she stirred her cup of hot chocolate. We were both silent for a moment; she sipped her chocolate and I drank my milk. I couldn't quite imagine a child in my life. It was invisible and therefore unreal to me, but there was also a chance that it would simply never be born. We didn't know each other very well, but even though I'd already made my plans, which she and the child weren't a part of, no more than I was a part of hers, I liked her. There wasn't supposed to be any epilogue to our visit to the greenhouse. Should I tell her that I was sorry, that I regretted having invited her to see the tomato plants in the greenhouse and apologize for not having done anything to prevent the child's conception? Would she maybe be offended by that? Or should I tell her that I wouldn't run away from my responsibilities for the child that was growing inside her, whether I liked it or not?

—When is the baby due? I asked her.

—Around the seventh of August.

That's Mom's birthday. I felt I didn't have an awful lot to say on the matter. Maybe I should have asked my friend, while she was sitting opposite me at the table, what she thought about all this, how she felt about having a child with me. But instead she said:

—I don't really expect anything of you.

This triggered mixed feelings in me, that she should have decided in advance not to expect anything of me.

—Still, I'm sure I could become fond of a child, I said.

She sipped her chocolate and wiped the cream off her lips; she was as skinny as a reed.

—Wouldn't you like something to eat? I said, handing her the menu. There was mainly a selection of soups and sandwiches, but I also spotted fried catfish and pointed it out to her.

—I wouldn't be able to keep it down, she said.

At that moment I should have maybe asked myself what kind of mother my child was getting, but I was somehow unable to connect to this woman's child; I couldn't build that bridge between the child and me. I couldn't place my deeds into any context, connect cause and effect, hadn't entertained the possibility that my seed might fall on fertile soil and take up residence inside the woman who was now sitting in front of me, stirring a cup of hot chocolate.

In fact, there was nothing I could do but wait for her phone call to come and have a look at the baby. It was difficult to imagine that the child would ever have any need for me, whether her mother would ever call me to come and babysit while she went to the cinema, presumably with the child's stepfather? The child had to be born first.

—I've got to dash, said the genetics student, pulling up the zipper of her blue hooded parka. I have to go to a lecture on faulty chromosomes.

I finished the glass of milk and paid for it and the chocolate. She held out her hand to me and I held out mine. You just had to look at her running across the street and hopping on the bus to see that she'd manage, there was nothing to feel guilty about.

Twenty-four

—Didn't you want to get to know the future mother of your child a bit better?

—Yeah, maybe, but it just didn't happen, we somehow went our separate ways.

—Didn't you see her again until the baby was born?

—Yeah, once, I say.

I bumped into her again at the end of April as she was lining up to buy a hot dog. I ran across the street and joined her in the queue; there was one man between us. Because I saw her first I had a moment to check her out before I said hi. She was in her blue parka with her thick, dark hair tied in a ponytail and a big scarf wrapped twice around her throat because it was a cold spring. She was visibly pregnant now; the baby had become a fact. I could feel my heart pounding and couldn't help thinking that there were now two hearts beating inside my half-night stand, but when I tried to revive the memory of our visit to the greenhouse, there were few images other than those of the leaves projected against her stomach.

I heard her order a hot dog with everything except raw onion and a little remoulade, and I remember thinking that then the baby was also having a hot dog with everything except raw onion and that it was being nourished by her, even though its eyes might turn out to be like mine.

I gave the man a chance to serve her before I greeted her by stepping in front of her and just saying hi.

—Hi. She smiled at me with her hot dog in one hand and seemed surprised to see me, shy even. My child's mother and I were two individuals who now greeted each other on street corners. I asked how she was, but she had just bitten into her hot dog so I waited while she chewed and swallowed. It was clumsy of me to throw a question at her just when her mouth was full, and she tried to chew as fast as she could, while I stared straight at her. Then she wiped some invisible mustard off the corner of her mouth. She had a beautiful mouth. She told me that being pregnant was like being seasick for months on end. I understood her completely and felt partly responsible. I was between sea trips myself, as it happened. She added that the worst of it was now over and that she was starting her exams.

She occasionally glanced at her half-eaten hot dog, as we stood facing each other and I had a direct view of a trickle of mustard beginning to solidify. While she adjusted the violet scarf around her neck, she handed me her hot dog and I held it in my left hand and my own in my right hand. I was minding something for her, the way friends do. She didn't look like an expectant mother; there was nothing particularly motherly about her, she looked just like a girl who was starting to take her exams and was deeply immersed in essays.

I handed her back her hot dog, and she was looking at me so I involuntarily ran my hand through my thick mop of hair; I wanted to create a good impression. I didn't know if she ever thought of me; she was probably just trying to work out what the child would look like. It wasn't easy being a red-haired boy.

—Do you know the sex yet? I asked.

—No, she answered, but I have a feeling that it's a boy.

For a split second, I thought I had a brief flash of myself walking a boy in a blue playsuit and a blue balaclava. I was either picking him up at his mother's or returning him; I couldn't fill in the time gap between those two things. We might have been feeding bread to the ducks—the pond was frozen, and we stood by a hole in the ice where the ducks were squabbling. In the vision I was holding the boy's hand, I wasn't going to lose a child I had been entrusted with for half a day down some hole in the ice or anything like that. Nevertheless, I found it difficult to construct a scene out of something that hadn't become a reality yet. Although I wouldn't be bringing up my child with its mother—I tested out the sound of those words in my mind, *mother of my child*—I wasn't a shit and I felt like telling her that she could count on me, and telling her I could take the boy to his gym classes and we could be friends.

—All the best with your exams, I said as we were saying good-bye. All I could do now was wait for Anna to call me one night to ask me to come and see the baby.

—The only thing I could do was wait for the baby to be born, I say to my traveling companion, and just leave it at that.

Twenty-five

I wondered how long I could wait before I told Dad about the child who would probably be coming into the world on Mom's birthday in August and how I should announce it to him. I was twenty-one years old and living at home; Dad was fifty-five when he had his first and only children, his twins, Jósef and me. The strangest thing was that my greatest worry was having to tell Dad the expected date of birth. Which bits should I divulge and which bits should I keep to myself about the conception and birth of the child? Should I just spill it out over dinner, out of the blue, casually even, like it was no big deal to have a child with a woman you didn't know, or should I take a more formal approach and tell him that I needed to have a little chat with him in private, as if there were anyone else in the house, and sit down on the sofa and turn off the radio news to underline the importance of this inevitable event? I felt like I was about to reveal material to the electrician from a novel that I hadn't read yet, and therefore I honestly couldn't think of any way of making it interesting. I was also afraid of disappointing him, that he might think I was finally going to tell him of my decision to study botany.

When I finally thought I'd found the right moment to tell Dad the news, my friend phoned to tell me that she was on her way to the maternity ward because she was about to give birth. She said she would wait for me, and I thought I sensed a certain vulnerability in her voice, as if she were about to cry.

It was ten thirty on a Friday night, the sixth of August.

—She called me when the baby was coming, I say to the actress.

It's been three hours since we left and we're still in the forest. I see my traveling companion digging into her drama student bag again, looking for her red lunch box.

I must admit I was totally surprised that my friend called me before the baby was born; up until that moment I hadn't even expected the baby to necessarily be born at all. I dove under the shower and then ironed the only white shirt I had; that was my contribution to the birth, to be in a white, ironed shirt like at Christmas. Apart from that I didn't know what role Anna expected me to play in the birth. I felt I was on my way to an exam I hadn't studied for. Suddenly Dad appeared beside the ironing board, and I quickly told him that I was expecting a child with the friend of a friend of mine.

—D'you remember Thorlákur? I ask.

His reaction took me somewhat by surprise; he almost looked happy, then he took the iron and wanted to finish ironing the shirt for me.

—I never really expected to experience the joy of becoming a grandfather, he said, your mother and I weren't even sure you were that way inclined.

I didn't ask him what he meant by "that way inclined," but allowed him to help me put on my shirt, as if I were a little boy on his way to his first Christmas ball. He asked me if wanted to borrow a tie from him.

—No thanks.

The moment triggered a memory in him.

—Your mother practically filled up the whole orange kitchen unit in the last weeks she was pregnant with you two brothers, so I avoided going into the kitchen when she was

there. The apartment wasn't big and we were always bump-
ing into each other; there was no way of getting past her. I felt
as if I were one too many, as if the apartment just wasn't big
enough for the two of you and me.

Twenty-six

A short moment later I feel the need to place more cards on the table.

—I assisted at her birth, I say to the actress, knowing full well that my linguistic skills won't allow me to elaborate any further. It's as if someone else is talking through me about my private affairs to the girl.

My traveling companion clearly approves.

—Really? She looks at me with a mixture of puzzlement and admiration. Admiration, though, seems to be the dominant expression.

Even though I was no substitute for the midwife or anything like that, I was certainly present at my daughter's birth. And I wasn't left unmoved either.

The corridor was flooded in milky light. I didn't feel unwelcome, but at the same time I wasn't needed; my role in the child's conception had already been completed nine months earlier. Anna was in a white hospital gown that stretched over her taut belly, and she was wearing white socks. She seemed distant and anxious, as if she couldn't quite handle the situation.

The midwife gave me a warm welcome and I smiled at Anna. I knew how difficult this was for her and pitied her terribly; now I felt I was all to blame. I wanted to apologize, to tell her how sorry I was and that I'd never intended for this to happen to her. Instead, though, I just did what I was told and sat still on the chair that was placed by her bedside and patted the back of the hand of the future mother of my child. Two black ravens were perched on the ledge on the other side of the window, and the women spoke to each other in hushed tones, while Anna lay in silence on her side, clutching a white pillow in her arms.

I couldn't fathom how it had ever occurred to the mother of my child to have me present; we barely knew each other. I felt totally superfluous, but fortunately it all happened quite fast; I didn't have to watch my friend agonizing for days on end. The birth went smoothly and swiftly, and the baby was born shortly after midnight on Friday the seventh of August, two hours after I arrived at the hospital. It was a girl, and she was gluey red and cried briefly, just while she filled her lungs with air and wriggled her limbs in all directions. Then she quieted down, grew calm, and looked around, tranquil pearly eyes emerging from the bowels of the earth. There was a faint glow in her deep blue eyes, as if they still belonged to the other world.

—What was it like to be at the birth of the child? my companion in the car asks.

—It was surprising.

—What was surprising?

—You think about death. Having a child gives you the certainty that you're going to die one day.

—Weird guy, she says.

What makes her say that? Unless I misheard her. My brain is having problems dealing with so many things at once—translating, stringing together unfamiliar words, and trying to work out what extra meanings they might have. My traveling companion, on the other hand, expresses herself effortlessly. I don't have the guts to ask her what she meant by *weird*. So instead I say:

—Weird girl yourself.

I didn't know what was going through Anna's head, but personally I was a little bit surprised that it was a girl. The midwife showed me how to hold the slippery baby and weave a little cocoon around its minuscule body. She gave off a slightly sweet smell, like vanilla caramel. My daughter also seemed to treat my amateurish attempts with understanding and looked at me with her big, alert eyes veiled in a mist, totally calm. At first sight, she seemed hairless, but when her head was wiped, a film of light yellow down appeared.

—My daughter had little hair when she was born, I say to my traveling companion, like some lawyer reopening an old case because some new evidence has been produced.

If it hadn't been for the smell and the feel of the baby's soft body, it might have all seemed very unreal to me, like watching a film. I tried to show my child's mother some moral support and patted her shoulder. Her eyes were burning as if she'd just been through a life experience that I could never understand. The baby—I tried out the words *my daughter*—was incredibly tiny and beautiful, like a porcelain doll. The midwife who had wrapped the baby in a towel had also said she was beautiful. Her words were mainly directed at the mother, and then she gave me this slightly bewildered look, as if she were trying to figure out where I fit in with the child. Anna held the baby in her arms, but it was as if her mind were elsewhere, as if she'd done her duty now and wanted to go to sleep. Then she turned to me and said:

—She's just like you. And then she handed me the bundle, as if to confirm that the child definitely wasn't from her side of the family and that her contribution had been first and foremost to nourish my daughter with the right vitamins and then go through the inevitable process of bringing her into the world. It was two o'clock in the morning and I was wondering when might be the right time to take my leave. I could well understand that Anna was tired, but the baby's gaze was fixed on me and I longed to hold her a little bit longer. I wanted to tell the child's mother that she could have a rest now and fall asleep even and that I would just sit there a bit longer, alone with the baby, that's if that was all right with her.

As I was practicing holding the child, her mother seemed to be sizing me up. She looked as if she either wanted to cry or just vanish from the scene, leaving me alone with the child. I was the one who started crying in the end, not the mother. She looked at me in puzzlement, as did the midwife and medical student.

—People are often overwhelmed by feelings when they have a baby, particularly their first one, the midwife explained. That's how she put it, overwhelmed by feelings.

—I cried, I say unflinchingly in the car. The drama student looks at me with interest. I give myself some extra points for not falling into the temptation of glorifying myself in the girl's eyes.

Even though we were, strictly speaking, two virtual strangers having a child together, the midwife strongly recommended that I stay with the mother and child in the hospital that night.

The room was equipped for fathers, too, their needs were also taken into account; there was an extra sofa bed. The baby slept in a Plexiglas cradle beside her mother's bed. The child's mother didn't raise any objections, but stared at me, as if she were trying to place me in her life, as if her body remembered something her mind couldn't quite recall. Because there was so little hair on my daughter's head, it was recommended that she wear a bonnet, the midwife explained to me.

—The body mainly cools down from the head, she said, and I thought I detected an apologetic tone as she was placing the pink bonnet on my daughter. Before clocking off her shift, she gave each of us booklets on family insurance and parental leave.

My child's mother dozed off as soon as her head hit the pillow, which was understandable, since she'd just brought a whole child into the world. She was both exhausted and aching. I would have been perfectly willing to say something beautiful to her, but she was too tired to listen. I imagined it must be strange to wake up on a Friday morning and go up to the hospital to give birth to a baby. I also would have liked to have been kind to her somehow, but just didn't know how to go about it. I felt it was almost an act of sacrilege for me, a fully grown man, to fall asleep in a bed in a maternity ward. I'd never slept in the same room as the mother of my child before, and had only spent enough time with her to conceive a child. It would have been out of the question for me to wander around the maternity ward in my underpants, or even my blue striped pajamas, garments the mother of my child had never seen me in. This wasn't a hotel room and we weren't lovers. An adult male who went to the toilet and then forgot to put the seat down had no place in this silk-soft world of breast-suckers and mothers, in this smooth downy nest.

Once the midwife was gone and Anna had fallen asleep for the night, I wheeled the cradle over to the sofa bed and bent over it to stare at the baby. I was alone with the child. She was awake and staring right back at me; my moment of carelessness made flesh was staring at me.

—The baby was awake and staring at me, I say to my fellow passenger in the car. We're finally out of the woods, which are supplanted by fields of golden sunflowers that stretch for as far as the eye can see, giant yellow flower heads. It has started to rain.

I bent over so that my daughter could make out the outlines of my face and see her father. She was an incredibly beautiful child— of course, I didn't have much to compare her to, even though I'd caught fleeting glimpses of a few other startled newborns in the ward. They looked like old people, with their red-violet flesh, all wrinkled with apprehension and burdened by the new life that had just begun. My child—our child—was different. She seemed to neither resemble me nor her mother; she was unique somehow, a new issue—not that I'd had any preconceptions of what the baby would look like; on the contrary, I'd practically pushed any speculations of that kind out of my mind. I scrutinized the baby, drank her with my eyes.

Then I lifted the quilt, and my daughter stretched her legs and twinkled her toes as I examined her incredibly tiny foot. There was a lot of light around the child; I wondered whether it might have been coming from some material in the quilt cover.

—Welcome, I whispered gently, sticking my little finger into the baby's palm. I didn't undress but stayed up all night staring at the child, partly also because I didn't know when I would see her again. My daughter's mother and I weren't a couple, and I wasn't even sure I would meet my child's mother that often, although I would undoubtedly be welcome to visit the child we had together.

Anna was exhausted and slept all night, with her mouth slightly ajar, the sleep of the just. I kind of checked on her several times, though I refrained from exploiting my position and staring at her at length. But I adjusted her quilt, spreading it over her a bit better, and then rearranged our daughter's dwarf covers as well. That rounded off my tasks for the night. Mom also used to adjust my quilt when she was clearing up at night. It was the last thing I remembered before I fell asleep in the dark, Mom pulling the quilt over me; then she tidied up in the kitchen, closed the windows, turned off the lights, and called it a day. It was then that I realized I knew nothing about the family of my child's mother and that I hadn't even asked her about my child's grand-dad and granny. I couldn't very well walk up to the bed where she was sleeping, pale with her rosy cheeks and moist lips, bend over her, shake her shoulder, and ask:

—Who are your parents, Anna?

The drama student is all ears, wriggles in her seat, and sits up, waiting with bated breath to see if I can form another seven-word sentence:

—A newborn baby was staring at me, I repeat to her.

Then I bent all the way down to the baby and gently picked her up, as light as a feather, in her white frotté bodysuit, and carefully lay down on the pillow on the sofa bed with the baby in my arms, adjusting her as carefully as I could on my tummy and pulling the quilt over her. Her legs were in the fetal position, but I delicately pulled on one heel and then the other, and my daughter stretched out one leg herself and I felt it pressing against my belly button. Although I tried to breathe as lightly as I could, the baby rose and sank, like a baggy airbed; then I stroked her gently on the back until she fell asleep. I was very careful not to fall asleep myself.

Twenty-seven

The fresh new granddad asked whether he should collect Jósef at the community home to take him to see the baby. I told him how things were—that I barely knew the girl, that I hadn't put her into the family picture yet, hadn't even mentioned the brother who shared a birthday with me, hadn't spoken about my relationship with Mom—we weren't close, I told him, despite our one-off close encounter.

—We're not a couple, Dad, I say.

—You're not going to shirk your responsibilities, Lobbi lad? Your mother wouldn't have liked that.

He felt this was a good cue to revive some old memories of when his twins were born.

—They didn't know what was wrong with Jósef at first, but they put him in the incubator because he was weak. And because you were his twin brother they put you into the incubator with him for the first twenty-four hours. When I bent over the pair of you I saw that you had taken your brother's hand, just a day old and already taking care of him.

He wasn't just implying that we were holding hands, but that I was already taking care of my two-hours-younger brother who had something wrong with him; he had embellished the memory with the benefit of hindsight.

—You took his hand. Your brother slept for most of his first year. You, on the other hand, were wide awake and observing the world.

That's how he set us brothers up, as opposites.

—You started walking when you were ten months old, while Jósef was still sleeping. Your mom spent a lot of time with you. I was more with your brother. We divided you between us. You and your mom liked to chat a lot together, and Jósef and myself were quiet together. It suited us all that way.

Then the electrician was offering to buy a stroller for the grandchild and outdoor overalls and leggings or anything else she might be short of. Once more, Mom had the last word.

—Your mother wouldn't have had it any other way.

He insisted I buy three of everything: three bodysuits with buttons on the shoulder, three pairs of stockings, three pajamas with different patterns, elephants, giraffes, and teddy bears. He also wanted me to buy a baby carriage and outdoor overalls. Then Dad pulled out his wallet.

—Your mother wouldn't have had it any other way.

—She's just like you when you were her age, Dad said when he saw his granddaughter. I thought it was only grannies who said things like that.

—Twenty-four hours old? Do you remember what I looked like when I was twenty-four hours old? I asked the brand-new granddad.

—She's the spitting image of your mother, he confirmed. As if Mom and I were one.

He was hoping the child would be named after Mom; I could see it when he was looking at the baby, he was looking for Mom.

—I've got no say in the name, Dad, I said. It would be different if we were living together. Besides, the child's mother's name is Anna, just like Mom, so she'd be naming her after herself.

He didn't understand that point of view.

—Her name is Flóra Sól, my daughter, I say to the drama student.

—Cute, she says. Then we just sit in silence. We haven't far to go now.

Twenty-eight

The landscape is changing; there are round hills ahead, and mountains appear in the distance. The sunflower fields are behind us now and we're back into thick woodlands. The road is wet, so I focus on my driving; we're both silent. Some blinking blue lights appear ahead of us, so I slow down and shift into first gear as I approach the luminous plastic cones that have been placed in the middle of the road. A police officer in a rainproof fluorescent vest stands in front of the car and signals me to drive up along the edge of the road onto the gravel, passing a car that is missing its front half, as if it had suddenly been severed in two. There's a trail of oil on the road. I drive painstakingly slowly past the scene of the accident; the front of the car has vanished as if it has been swallowed by the forest. I spot another fluorescent-vested policeman off the side of the road and see him lift a leg off the ground; it has a man's shoe on it and black socks. He's holding the leg right in front of my car and uses his other hand to signal me to drive on. As I drive past, I see the other half of the car and a semi-view of the bodies still sitting upright inside it, an elderly man and woman, tastefully dressed, all spruced-up in fact, sitting erect, side by side, like a couple that has been sitting silently at the dining table together for decades on end. No trace of blood, their ashen faces seem unscathed, like dummies in a wax museum. Most shocking of all, I feel no repulsion, and yet I'm not an insensitive person. Instead, I very calmly try to picture myself in the lives of this couple on the road, as if I were trying to solve an important riddle, but no matter how I approach the enigma, I just can't picture myself sitting beside the same woman for decades on end, whether it be in a car or at a dining table.

What if I were to meet the same fate on this road? If I, say, crashed the car into a tree and the windshield smashed all over us and we, the actress and I, were to die side by side? What would the mother of my child think when the news appeared? Perhaps some traces of us would remain in the woods, the soaked final scene of *A Doll's House* maybe? The rescuers always overlooked something. Or, just as likely, the pages would be placed in a plastic bag and Dad would receive these mysterious pages he wouldn't understand.

I look at the girl. She's sitting with her hands on her lap, her eyes full of tears.

—There now, I say touching her shoulder.

—There now, I say again and stroke her cheek.

Now that we've witnessed the results of a fatal accident together, one could say that we have a shared experience behind us. What's more, I've already shared the experience of my child's birth with her, so, all in all, our joint experiences span six hours, sitting side by side in the car, having covered the two most important events on the path of human existence—birth and death, the beginning and end. If she were to suddenly ask me out of the blue in these last sixty miles of the journey if I wanted to sleep with her I wouldn't say no.

When I turn back onto the national highway, I drive past the stationary van that drove down this forest road in the wrong place at the wrong time. Maybe the driver was looking for a radio station that played light classical music. Through the rearview mirror I can still see the glow of blinking blue police lights in the rain.

A brief moment later, I have to pull up on the side of the road again, into a clearing in the forest, this time to throw up the meat sandwich I ate earlier today. I don't feel well and if I hadn't just had my appendix out, I might have thought a new fit of appendicitis was developing.

I kill the engine and we both step out of the car. I'm in my white shirt and I'm cold. Crickets can be heard and all kinds of small creatures, and the scent of the undergrowth is overwhelming in the drizzle.

—There now, she says, it's all over.

I feel it's appropriate to walk about ten yards away from the car to throw up the remains of the sandwich. Ten to fifteen yards, that's about the same distance that members of captured rebel forces are required to walk when they are escorted from a truck before being executed.

—There now, she says again when I've finished throwing up, stroking my shirtsleeve. Then she takes my hand and leads me into the woods.

—Let's just get some air while you're recovering.

This is her home territory; maybe she's been here before with the owner of the inn, her father, to shoot a stag. I'm shivering because I'm in my shirt, like a man strolling straight out of a concert into the woods in his concert shirt.

We forge our path through clusters of dead twigs, bending branches full of dewy juices, until we finally sit against the trunk of an oak tree that is probably a thousand years old. You only have to peel the bark a little to find it rife with life, an entire community of ants.

—Have you always had that name? she asks.

—What do you mean? Do you change your names as you grow older?

She laughs. I laugh with her.

I pick three horse chestnuts and stick them in my pocket; then I remove a light green venous leaf from the actress's shoulder and pluck several straws off her before we sit in the car again.

Twenty-nine

When I reach the end of the journey with the girl, she places a hand on my shoulder and directs me into the town I had originally intended to bypass. She tells me that, in addition to the drama school, the town also hosts a clown's school and famous circus, as well as being the producer of a renowned blue cheese. I turn five times to the right until I come to the building that she lives in, close to the famous historical center.

—There, she says, bursting into a sudden flurry of activity, we've arrived.

It's raining on the windshield, and in some odd way it feels like I'm breaking up with a girlfriend or something, even though I've no direct experience of anything like that. She wriggles in her seat, with her hand still on my shoulder.

—Are you in a hurry? she asks. Do you have to get to your destination by a specific time?

—No, not exactly, but I have a long way to go yet, I add, to give her a more assertive answer. I'm guarding myself against surprise questions, potential requests; women often have plans and organize things ahead of time without you even realizing it.

—No, I was just going to ask you if you wanted to stay, she says. I share an apartment with another two girls who are with me at the school, so there's plenty of room for you, too.

I ponder on whether there can be any danger in accepting the invitation to stay, whether it might affect my future plans. People who pop up in your life for just a brief moment can have a greater impact than those who sit there for years on end. Experience has taught me what an insidious and fateful effect coincidences can have.

—Seriously, she says, adjusting her hair and tucking a lock under her ribbon. It's getting dark anyway so it'll be night soon.

—Yeah, thanks, I say, deciding to share the apartment with the three actresses. In any case I'll be gone before they wake up.

—There's just one thing, she says. My roommates are vegetarians, I hope you don't mind. For the dinner, I mean. We'll probably have spinach lasagna tonight.

As we're stepping out of the car, she suddenly says:

—What did you call that plant that's like a trampoline again?

Thirty

I do my best not to wake up the girls while I'm preparing to leave. They don't have to be at school until the afternoon. Before I go, I fold the sheets and blanket and place them on the mattress on the floor under a poster of a movie star in a shapely black dress, with drooping almond eyes, eyelashes like butterflies, and black tresses. Then I write a few lines to the three tenants to thank them for the fun evening and spinach lasagna and stick the note between the unwashed glasses on the kitchen table. So far chance seems to have thrown quite a few companions my way on this journey through the rainy forest, such as this actress and her friends. Dawn is at the point of breaking when I dash out to the trunk and fetch one of the two foreign rose plants with three pink buds, and then stick it beside my farewell note on the kitchen table. There seems to be a fair deal of chaos in these actresses' lives, which is clearly reflected in the leftovers and dirty dishes in the kitchen. On second thought, I take the dishes and glasses and place them in the sink, wipe the table clean, and tidy up a bit so as to highlight the rose a bit better.

Although my mind occasionally drifts back to the movie star as I slowly drive the Opel over the mountain road and then down into the lowlands, I feel it's good to be alone again; the physical proximity of a girl can throw a wrench into the works. For even though I don't maybe think of sex all the time, I'm feverishly trying to work out the connection between myself and my body, as well as my body and the bodies of others. The next time I stop to consult the map, I move the rose cuttings out of the trunk and place them on the floor beside me. By now they've survived a flight, a stay in the hospital in sterilized plastic glasses, and fairly rudimentary storage conditions in the trunk and backseat of the car, for what will soon be over twelve hundred miles.

Since Dad is constantly worried about me, I give him a call from a phone booth at a gas station once I've crossed the border. When he's finished asking me about the weather and the traffic conditions on the roads, he tells me that seven depressions have crossed the country in about as many days. Then he tells me that the halibut soup was a great success and that he's now thinking of tackling Icelandic haggis.

—Just like your mom made it.

—The haggis season is another six months away.

—I just wanted to tell you well in advance. I think we need to uphold your mother's traditions. Not least for Jósef.

I've no recollection of Jósef ever taking part in the haggis preparation, but Mom let me sew the sheep's stomachs from when I was nine.

—This renovation mania is just something else, he then adds.

—How do you mean?

—Thórarinn, Bogga's son, keeps on changing things in his apartment. As soon as something is two years old it has to be replaced. This renovation mania just isn't natural. Like, there can't be the slightest trace of age on anything. You could almost convince yourself that you could avoid dying if you spent your whole life replacing cables and fittings, says the electrician who still has the same light blue kitchen unit that he put together when Mom first moved into the house.

—You're not short of pocket money, are you, Lobbi?

—No, I'm fine.

—And you're not lonely on your journey?

—No, no.

—And people are helpful?

—Yeah, yeah, people are helpful.

In fact it's true. People are incredibly helpful. I'm inclined to think that humanity is, broadly speaking, good and honorable, when given a chance, and that people, on the whole, do their best. If the person I ask hasn't heard of the place I'm looking for or doesn't know the way, he still tries to give me some directions to continue. At worst it might mean going astray in the mountains for a few hours because people can't stop themselves from being helpful. Nevertheless, I've managed to cross three borders in the Opel without any hiccups since I dropped off the girl, eat various types of pâté and chocolate when I'm hungry, and sleep three nights with a roof over my head in about as many countries. Because I'm traveling alone I often have to stop to check the map. The only problem is that the map doesn't tell you how steep the roads are, just the distances in miles and you wouldn't want to be suffering from vertigo driving up the final thirty miles of a winding mountain road. The curves are terrifyingly sharp, and I thank god for the mist that prevents me from seeing the bottom of the valley below. In fact, it isn't until I reach my destination that I realize there's also a road beneath me in the valley. There's very little traffic; I only meet one white car in the final miles up to the village.

Thirty-one

The village is perched on a rock spur and I immediately spot the monastery on top of the cliff. It's hard to believe that there's a garden up there that is referred to in every handbook on the cultivation of roses since the Middle Ages.

The monastery is severed in two by a horizontal stripe of yellow mist that makes it look like it's hovering over its earthly foundations. The streets are so narrow that the sky is nothing but streaks above them. They're almost vertical, and I don't fancy driving the car any farther, so I take out my backpack and the box of rose cuttings and start walking up the hill. It's a good job my luggage is light. The exceptionally vivid colors of the buildings make me realize, after walking just a few yards, that I've stumbled into my brother Jósef's universe of colors—the pink of his shirt, mint green of his tie, violet of his sweater, and soft brown cheese color of his diamond waistcoat besiege me from about as many facades. Hydrangea and dahlias in ornate ceramic pots line the path up the hill, leading to the only level street at the very top. A church is perched at the end of it, framed against a blue light, with the monastery's guesthouse beside it—the place I'm supposed to report to.

I'm quick to find my bearings and it's easy to locate everything. There seems to be one of everything in this town, one guesthouse, one restaurant, one barbershop, one post office, one bakery, one butcher, and one beggar. The only exception are the churches, which abound on every corner, sometimes with even two or three of them huddled together; I've never seen so many churches crammed into such a small area. Everything, apart from the inhabitants, seems a thousand years old. I hold the box of plants in my arm and notice some of the locals peeping. By the time I've reached the top of the village, after a twenty-minute walk, I could well believe that I've already met half of the population. I catch a whiff of sauces bubbling in pots. Many are also finishing their shopping and carrying large bundles of leeks and celery in their arms. Incomprehensible words assail my ears, but I'm carrying a book in my backpack that should teach me how to get by in this dying dialect. I fleetingly check out some of the women I meet on my path, of varying ages. Before I know it, I've worked out a formula and projected it against the light violet facade of the guesthouse. If the fifty/fifty rule applies, one can expect three hundred fifty of the seven hundred inhabitants of this village to be women, and about thirty of those are likely to be in my age group, give or take five years.

The monk, Father Thomas, welcomes me at the entrance in a gray knitted sweater with a V-neck and cable pattern. He says he's been expecting me and that my room has been cleaned and the bed made. I'm in the blue sweater Mom knit, which has a similar cable pattern; I could turn this into a topic for conversation but don't feel it's appropriate at this early stage of our acquaintance-ship. Instead he asks me what language I would like to speak, offering me a selection to choose from, which throws me slightly.

—I used to be in linguistics, he says, languages are a hobby of mine.

I dare to ask him how many he speaks. He says he speaks nineteen quite well, has a fair knowledge of another fifteen, and a basic grasp of several others.

—Because of their kinship, he adds. Once you've got eleven languages under your belt it's easy to add a new one.

They don't get many guests at this time of the year, however, and my letter and interest in the garden had surprised him.

—Most of the guests come to look at the manuscripts, he says, grabbing a bottle of yellow liquid from a glass case in the hall and pouring it into two glasses.

—So we only have two heated rooms at the moment, you get one and I'm in the other. You can eat in the monastery when you're in the garden; there's soup at midday and a meal in the restaurant next door in the evenings. We have an account there. If you start on Monday, there's celery soup upstairs. I imagine you'll want to have a look around tomorrow; there's a beautiful church here with old paintings and beautiful stained-glass windows in the chancel.

He hands me another glass. I'm shivering after the journey.

—Welcome. As I was saying, we were somewhat surprised by your interest in the garden. Can you grow anything in your native country? Roses can hardly spring out of rocks. As I mentioned in the letter, the garden has lost some of its former glory. But if you feel you can work on it and even partly revive the rose grove, as you were saying, we have no objections to that.

Father Thomas eyes the box of plants I have carefully put down beside me.

—Brother Matthew has been tending to it on his own, but you can take over from him; he's grown weary of gardening and has spoken of his wish to work in the scriptorium like the others. There are countless manuscripts that need to be classified.

Father Thomas hands me the key to room eight and heads up the stairs.

—I live in room seven next door. You're welcome to pop in for another glass of lemon vodka when you've unpacked.

❈

Thirty-two

I'm quite happy with the room. The walls are lily blue and there's a bed, table, chair, sink, and wardrobe with four wooden hangers. It doesn't take me long to hang up two sweaters and two pairs of trousers. I put my T-shirts, underpants, and socks on the shelf, and have now fully unpacked with the feeling that I'm here to stay. Once I've placed the plants on the windowsill, I go out into the corridor and knock on the door of number seven. I have to admit I'm surprised by what I see when Father Thomas opens the door. The walls are literally covered in shelves crammed with videotapes right up to the ceiling. There's an old TV set in the middle of the floor with two chairs in front of it and also a desk on which there are two neat towers of tapes, a thick book which I imagine to be the Bible, and several other volumes and a pen stand.

He notices me staring at the tapes.

—Yes, you've guessed it, I'm a bit of a film buff, although I never go to the cinema. My acquaintances from around the world know of this weakness of mine and have sent me some precious films over the years; I have about three thousand now. There are movies from all over the world in here, in many languages, everything really except Hollywood movies. I'm bored by war heroes and all that artificial gimmickry, says Father Thomas, drawing out a chair for me and inviting me to sit.

Then he apologizes and says that he can only just about handle basic text in my mother tongue, but that he has no experience of actually speaking it; he's probably only ever seen one film from my country.

—But it was beautiful, he says. Very unusual. Very green grass. Big skies. Beautiful death.

I discover that Father Thomas watches films in their original language without subtitles.

—It's very good practice, he says. Then I've got my books in the monastery, I've also got a room there. Here I can watch films. Some people have a cat, I watch movies.

Father Thomas stands up, pats me once on the shoulder, fetches the lemon vodka bottle, and fills the glasses.

—You're welcome to come over if you fancy watching a film. I normally watch a movie every night. Over the past few weeks I've been looking at some forgotten directors.

He grabs a video case and brandishes it in the air:

—The special thing about this director is his deep sympathy for hapless people.

Thirty-three

The restaurant I have an account at for the evenings is beside the guesthouse; everything is beside everything here. The woman is aware of who I am; Father Thomas has announced my arrival. It's actually just a small room with four tables and tablecloths. It has a rather special smell to it, both sweet and acerbic, like shellfish and rose water. The woman receives me from the kitchen, enveloped in a deep-fry mist and brandishing a spatula that's dripping with fat in her hand and which she now points at a table to tell me where to sit. I can see into the kitchen through the corner of my eye, where she is standing over the stove and slowly lowering the fish into the boiling fat. A brief moment later she raises the fish again, sizzling in a crunchy golden brown batter—crispy calamari—scoops them on my plate, slices some lemon with a razor-sharp knife, casually chucks that on my plate as well, and hands it to me. The woman gives off a scent of rose water through the frying vapors. Later she dumps a bowl of vanilla pudding in front of me and pours some hot caramel sauce over it from a jug.

Once I've finished eating I can go off to take a look at the village. It's actually starting to get dark, but nevertheless I take two trips up and down the main street. After two rounds I'm already starting to meet the same people again. The street is bustling with life. I imagine all the villagers stroll up and down this main street after dinner. The language is totally alien to me. I literally don't understand a single word; it all goes over my head.

My perception of the passersby as mere bodies disturbs me, and if it doesn't change it could become a real barrier to me developing any normal communication with these people and prevent me from learning their language. I carefully make sure I don't bump into anyone, though; I wouldn't know how to apologize to anyone in this new language. Mom was all into physical contact and always held some part of me when we were talking together. I found it difficult to stand still as a kid, always on the go.

—You're so restless and sprightly, she might have said.

I think I must have established eye contact with about eight women on my four strolls up and down the main street, with maybe one or two of them that I could think of sleeping with, if the opportunity were to present itself. These thoughts are more like precocious impulses, however, like faulty fireworks that refuse to go off.

In the square in front of the church, two steps away from the guesthouse, there's a phone booth. I decide to see if it works and find out how Dad's doing and just let him know I'm still in one piece.

Talking to Dad isn't easy. I've barely said hello to him and he's already worried about the price of the call and starting to say good-bye to me.

—Are you all right there, Lobbi?

—Yeah, fine, I just wanted to let you know I've reached my destination.

He doesn't beat about the bush.

—Do you not like the town?

—No, it's fine, a bit remote maybe, but I've got my own room.

—Is it a reliable room, Lobbi?

For a moment I ponder on what Dad might mean by a "reliable room," if it's in a solidly constructed building with a secure lock or that kind of thing. Whether it can withstand an earthquake maybe? He rewords his question:

—Is the landlord trustworthy? I hope he's not trying to con a young foreigner out of his hard-earned money made from braving the elements in the clutches of the sea?

—No, no, it's fine. I'm staying in a guesthouse owned by the monastery and have free food and lodging. The priest lives in the room next door.

—Is he a trustworthy person?

—Yes, Dad, very trustworthy, he's very interested in films and speaks every language under the sun.

—So you're not homesick then?

—No, not at all. Of course, I've only been here three hours.

—You're not broke yet?

—No, no, I have everything I need.

—You still have your mother's inheritance money.

—Yeah, I know that.

—I looked in on your daughter and her mother the other day.

—Really?

—You don't mind me popping in to see my granddaughter?

—No, I say.

I feel a bit uneasy about it, but can't say I'm against it.

—She's beautiful, the little girl, the spitting image of your mother. Same birthday.

He doesn't mention the date of her death.

—There's a long history of blond hair in the family. Your mother told me that your great grandfather was very blond, with golden locks. They were slow to change color, which gave him a boyish look, with delicate facial features well into middle age. So the girls didn't really fancy him much, not until later in life.

—So my daughter takes after her father's side of the family?

—Yeah, you could say that.

Once I'm in bed, under clean sheets with a book about the language that's spoken around here, I feel terribly lonely. To be honest, I don't know what possessed me to come to this forsaken village. I adjust my pillow and lie down so that I can see the black night through the window. It's a full moon as far as I can make out. I check out the celestial vault: as to be expected, the moon is terrifyingly big and too close. My home stars have vanished from the sky and aren't shining anywhere; they've been replaced by shooting stars and unknown constellations, new incomprehensible patterns in the black firmament.

Then I start to make out a peculiar sound coming through the headrest, an engine noise like that of a boat, very muffled voices, a silence, and then people talking rapidly together in disagreement. It's followed by beautiful music. I sit up and try to locate the sound, I'm pretty sure it's coming from the room next door. I prick up my ears but can't identify the language; I think it could even be Chinese. In any case it's clear that Father Thomas is watching some gem of a movie in his room.

Thirty-four

I must have fallen asleep too early because it's only six a.m. and I'm wide awake. Resounding peals are announcing the early morning mass, and I can see the centuries-old bell right outside my window. What seemed like a quiet guesthouse turns out to be located right next door to the main building of the church.

I slip into my trousers and sweater. I might as well go out, since I'm awake anyway. I pull up the top of my hooded sweater and step into the violet dawn. There isn't a soul in sight, and the café is closed. A peculiar red-bluish mist hangs over the village. I walk toward the source of the ringing coming from within the building that I now realize is attached to the guesthouse. The church entrance looks like any other door on the street. The facade gives nothing away of what lies within. In retrospect, I think the beggar was kneeling there somewhere in the dark last night. Did I give him some coins or not? Did I use all my change to call Dad from the phone booth or did I give it to the beggar then? It's suddenly important to me.

I glance around and there's no one around. I squeeze through the door where I follow a maze of corridors and twisted passageways until I reach another door. I open it and suddenly find myself in a large church; the stone gives off a cold, moist smell and an enormous space opens up before me, an entire vault of colored lights that makes me gasp and remove my hood. It's like stepping through the narrow mouth of a cave and discovering an entire palace of stalactite and Iceland spar. I step out of the twilight of the alleyway straight into the sunrise in the church.

A mass is beginning, and a shaft of sunrays tighten on the chancel in a glowing golden light. Father Thomas glances at me; there are another eleven monks in the church with him dressed in white robes. An agonizing Christ hangs on a dark wooden cross high above the altar, and colorful paintings adorn all the walls. I take one tour and look around. Even though I can't figure out all the scenes depicted in the paintings, I recognize some of the saints. I pause a moment in front of a statue of Saint Joseph and then move toward a painting of Mary on a throne with the baby Jesus. What draws my attention to it is that the infant has golden hair, three blond curls on its forehead, not unlike my daughter's, fresh out of the bath when I was saying good-bye to her and her mother. Examining the painting even closer, I can't help seeing other similarities between my daughter and the child in the picture: the shape of the face, the big bright eyes, the same flowery mouth, nose, chin; even the dimples are the same, no matter which way I look at it. The painting looks old; there's a crack in it and one of Mary's sleeves has probably recently been restored, the blue color isn't the same below the elbow.

When I step out of the church again, two tables have been set up outside the village café. I sit at one of them, and the owner brings me a pastry with some yellow custard in it for breakfast, which he tells me is a specialty of the region.

I combed through the village in half an hour yesterday so I can't really think of what I can do today. There obviously isn't much going on in the village on Sundays; people are eating at home and resting after their meals. So I decide to give Dad another call to see how he's doing. He's used to waking up at the crack of dawn and has finished fixing screeching hinges and gluing loose tiles at that hour of the morning. He might be surprised that I'm calling him two days in a row, but I make sure that my voice doesn't betray any doubts about the place and my position here, or he might start urging me to come home and go to university. When he's finished asking me about the weather and I've told him it's pretty much the way it was yesterday, except that instead of a yellow mist there was a bluish-red veil of mist this morning, he tells me the days are getting brighter back home.

—The day was two minutes longer today.

I'm suddenly tired of Dad. Before the spring arrives, another hundred twenty depressions will cross the country and Dad will be giving me reports on every single one of them.

—Yeah, and then it'll start to get dark again, Dad.

—If we survive that long.

—Yeah, if you survive that long.

—Your mother should never have gone before me, a young woman, sixteen years younger, fifty-nine years old, that's no age.

—No, she shouldn't have left before you.

We both shut up and I dig into my pocket for more coins. Then he tells me that he's been invited to Bogga's for glazed ham tonight.

—Right, is she doing OK?

—Fine, although I've never really been into glazed ham or pork in general.

—Have you turned into a Jew?

—Don't know what to bring her.

—Can't you give her some tomatoes? Doesn't she have four grown-up children?

—That's an idea, Lobbi.

He pauses a moment before asking me if I'm running short of cash.

—No, I don't need anything.

—You're not lonely, are you?

—No, no, not at all. I'm going to the garden tomorrow.

—The rose garden.

—Yeah, right, the rose garden.

—I imagine it's at least better than being at sea, says Dad. He seems to be unmoved by the fact that I've driven all this way, had a close shave with death at the beginning of my trip, and that I'm now on the threshold, so to speak, of one of the most famous rose gardens in the world, where one is likely to encounter the greatest variety of roses in one spot than any other place around the globe. It was Mom who showed me the first book about this garden when I was a kid, and practically every book I've read about rose cultivation ever since seems to refer to this remote monastic garden, far off the beaten track. Few of the authors knew the garden from personal experience, however, but rather through other written sources, and I've noticed that the wording is even taken directly from the descriptions written in the old manuscripts.

—Right you are, son. You just tell your dad if you're ever short of cash.

In some ways I'm more content with my lot now that I've spoken to Dad and it's killed my longing to go home.

Thirty-five

The monastery is within walking distance at the top of the hill and accessible from several steep paths from the village. Who would have expected a rose garden in this place, so high above sea level and on a rock? I can't see the garden at first because it's enclosed within the monastery walls on three sides and only open on the side facing away from the village. The hills are also terraced with the vineyards that produce the monks' wine. Brother Matthew receives me; he's supposed to show me around the garden and fill me in.

—Father Thomas told me about you and said that I would recognize you straight away, he says with a smile. He said you stand out in a crowd, tall with ginger hair. We're very happy to have you.

The most famous rose garden in the world is a shadow of its former self, as Father Thomas warned me three times. The paths and paving stones are buried under weeds, the rose beds seem to have grown together into a single tangle, and once upon a time there was a pond in the middle of the garden here and lawns with benches. Despite the uncultivated state of the garden all around me, I immediately recognize it from the pictures.

—Yes, that's right, the garden has been neglected and fallen into a state of disrepair, Brother Matthew explains. We've been concentrating on wine production and the library. We still have another thousand manuscripts that need to be classified. And our numbers have been shrinking in the monastery. The younger brothers of our order prefer to work on the

manuscripts than to be out in the garden; they mainly step outside to smoke, says Brother Matthew, who looks like he could
be in his eighties.

We walk around the garden; there are a number of things
that surprise me, and it turns out to be even bigger than I had
imagined. Even though it needs to be built up from scratch, I can
see how it can be restored. Most of the rose species are still there.
I can't resist the temptation to touch the plants, feel their soft
green leaves; I find no traces of lice.

—Yes, that's right, says Brother Matthew, most of the species
are still here. But you can't see them all because roses blossom
at different times of the year; in fact, there aren't many in bloom
right now, probably no more than seventy.

We break our way through the thick undergrowth along the
old path hidden below it, and farthest in the distance, I can make
out fruit trees that seem to encircle the garden.

—*Rosa gallica, Rosa mundi, Rosa centifolia, Rosa hybrida,
Rosa multiflora, Rosa candida.* Brother Matthew lists them off.

As I walk around the garden with Brother Matthew, this
magnificent celestial rose garden, as it's referred to in the old
books, gradually begins to take shape in my mind. I will have to
start by weeding it and pruning the plants, which could take me
up to two weeks if I work ten hours a day; then I'll have to thin
the soil and do some replanting to give the flowers enough elbow
room to grow in. I've already selected a sheltered and sunny spot
in my mind for the new species of rose I'm going to add. It may
not be very visible at first and it won't blossom straight away, but
this spot has the right conditions and light for a new unknown
rose species planted in fertile soil to grow. The plastic hospital
glasses are no longer to be trusted; you can't go on breeding life
in cotton wool forever. I decide not to delay bringing up the subject of the eight-petaled rose that I've left on the windowsill in the

guesthouse, and pull out a photograph of the rose in full blossom in the greenhouse.

—No, I'm not familiar with this species, says Brother Matthew after a moment's silence, I don't think there are any like that in our garden. It bears some resemblance to the rare white rose, *Rosa candida*, but the color is different, rather unusual. What did you say it was called?

—Eight-petaled rose. There are eight petals growing together at the base of the flower, then another eight around it, in triple layers; altogether there are twenty-four petals forming the bud, which is almost always dewy, I explain. It's true that it's related to the *Rosa candida*, except that this one isn't white. This one comes from a more resilient stock, probably the only of its kind in the world, I say. Although I've looked at many books about roses, I've never come across this species anywhere else.

—Very interesting, says Brother Matthew, unusual shape of the crown.

—And the stems have no thorns.

—Very interesting, he repeats, scrutinizing the photograph. Very peculiar color, extremely rare. It's neither pink nor violet. Violet red, wouldn't you say?

—Yes, exactly, I say, violet red.

—This is an unusually strong color that seems to spread all around it. Unless it's the film, is this Kodak? Brother Matthew asks.

He takes a few steps with the photograph in his hand and holds it up to one or two of the red pink rose buds for comparison.

—Like I say, I've never seen anything like it. You should show your eight-petaled rose to Brother Zacharias; he's ninety-three and he's been in the monastery for sixty-two years. He's actually started to lose his sight a little and we're not always too sure of how much he can see.

Then he says it's almost soup time, and suddenly remembers something before I even get a chance to mention the scent of my rose.

—We ordered some new boots for you. We felt we couldn't just give you the old boots that have been left unused in the shed for seven years. We also saw that they would be too small. It took them six weeks to get here. At first there was a mistake and they got sent to a monastery in Ireland, where it rains a lot.

He escorts me into a little shed in the garden. The boots are on the floor right inside the door; they're blue, glistening, and seemingly new, just like the ones I saw in my dream in the hospital.

—I hope they fit you, size ten and a half, isn't that what you said?

They can also lend me working clothes, trousers, a sweater, and gloves. I slip into the trousers; the legs reach down to my calves, and the arms on the sweater are just as short; the last person who worked in the garden obviously wasn't very tall.

—They haven't been worn in a long time, for seven years in fact, Brother Matthew explains, and they probably need to be washed.

The gardening tools are also kept in the shed. They have quite a good collection of implements, including saws and various types of clippers, although they probably haven't been used for ages. There are some tools there that I've never seen before; unlike any traditional implements I know and I can't imagine what they're used for.

—Brother Zacharias should be able to show you how they work, my guide tells me.

Finally, he tells me that it's only fair that I should know that not all the monks are fond of the rose garden. Some of them are allergic to plants, and others get sick from the bugs that the ivy roses carry through the windows.

—Brother Jacob asked me to tell you not to plant any more climbing plants by the eastern wall off the sleeping quarters, close to his cell.

After sharing celery soup with the monks, I spend half a day on my own in my new boots in the garden, looking around, sketching the rose beds, and making a work plan for the following days. Although I may have some unclear ideas about myself, I do, nevertheless, have the ability to organize things ahead of time. I also see a potential way of enlarging the vegetable patch. The soup at lunchtime wasn't bad, but I can see ways of increasing their variety of vegetables and creating a separate patch for some of the herbs that grow here.

Thirty-six

I've become a gardener among monks and see that I have enough work cut out for me for the next two to three months. Until then I don't have to think about my plans for the future or what I'll do at the end of it, whether I'll go home or stay here longer. I feel it's quite likely, though, that I won't have reached any conclusions about my life in two or three months' time. I feel good in the garden; it's good to use this isolation among the flower beds to explore my longings and wants, silent in the soil; I don't even have to know the language. I'm also completely free from all the prayer sessions; I'm just a simple gardener. Everything needs to be reorganized; I have to draw up a new plan on the basis of the old design and everything I can find in the ancient manuscripts.

The first week all goes into weeding and clipping my way through the rosebushes, thorn bushes actually; then I'll finally get to know the whole garden. Occasionally I spend short spells on the grass in my bare feet, but more often than not I'm in the blue boots.

I don't know how much I'm supposed to report to Father Thomas, who is my main contact with the monastery. He says they're giving me carte blanche, and I should trust my own instincts and insight into roses, I think he also said. When I explain my ideas, adjustments, and changes to him, he gives me approving nods and is quick to deal with the matter.

—We're very happy to have you, he says, and he seems to be satisfied with every suggestion I make, including the idea of creating a small lawn by the benches. As he's already told me himself, his main passion is movies and languages; in fact, I'm not sure the other monks have any great interest in the garden either. As Brother Matthew mentioned, most of them are immersed in the books, and their attention is mainly focused on putting some order to the collection of manuscripts.

I'm constantly discovering new species in the uncultivated growth—rose trees, rosebushes, climbing and winding roses, dwarf roses, and wild roses—big individuals on long branches or clusters of flowers, with a variety of shapes, scents, and colors. The scent in the garden is almost overwhelming and its colorfulness is quite unique: violet, lily blue, pink, white, gray, yellow, orange, and red. In fact, I need to organize the colors better and reorder them. It takes a lot of work to create a space for all the roses. After two weeks I've already identified and classified over two hundred species.

The monks give me free rein in the garden, but by the second week more of them are starting to come out to peep at my progress and sniff the roses. They've stopped throwing cigarette stubs into the flower beds and are generous in their praise when they see the changes. I have to admit that their appreciation of what I'm doing means something to me. I'm wondering if Brother Jacob will settle for a rhododendron bush instead of ivy.

Although I spend all day with the plants and think about the garden a lot, I nevertheless spend a considerable amount of time thinking about the body while I'm working in the soil. I don't even manage to completely shut off those thoughts during my meetings with Father Thomas. Bodies seem to crop up in certain parts of my mind at twenty-minute intervals, even though there's nothing specific in the environment that conjures them up. The fact that I've come here with a sincere longing to work in the flower beds and at the same time sort out my life a bit makes no difference.

When I'm studying grammar, the body isn't in the fore-
ground, but as soon as I try to form words the body appears
again, like a stain blotting through a white cloth. On the surface
we're talking about the garden; in my mind I'm wrestling with
my longings. I'm also afraid that Father Thomas might be able to
read my mind like an open book; he has that look, as if he's about
to burst into laughter.

—What do you think of that?

—Of what?

He looks at me in puzzlement.

—What we were just talking about. The ivy rose.

I can't get over how incredibly cheerful and quick to laugh
these monks are, despite their abstention from the pleasures of
the flesh. I try to picture myself as one of them, but even though
I'm currently leading a chaste existence, no matter how hard I
try to visualize myself among them, the white habit is either too
small or too big.

Thirty-seven

I normally wake up at the crack of dawn. Besides, it's impossible to sleep through the clatter of the bells, since the bed I sleep in is practically on the doorstep of the temple. Before going into the garden I have a local custard pastry for breakfast in the café, at lunchtime I have vegetable soup in the monastery, and in the evenings I dine in the restaurant next door. My second week is still mostly concentrated on pruning the rose plants, but also shaping the evergreen shrubs and bushes into various forms and patterns, spheres and cones, in accordance with the pictures in the old books. In addition to the roses and shrubs in the garden, there are oak trees, a grove with fruit and fig trees, and various other plants: fellowship roses, peace roses, fuchsia, Adam's beard, and Gloria Dei all grow in the same patch by the tool shed. More often than not I work solidly until darkness falls at around six.

When I get back to the guesthouse I have a shower, wash off the rose fragrance, and change clothes before going over for some deep-fried fish. I've also had fish soup from the woman next door, once grilled fish that was wrapped around a skewer with onion and bacon, and I've twice had squid. It took me a long time to cut the tentacles and chew them. After two weeks I feel a longing for meat. I wonder if it would be too presumptuous of me to ask the woman in the restaurant if she knows how to cook meat. I decide to take the matter up with Father Thomas instead. He scribbles four words on a note that I'm supposed to hand to the woman. After that I get meat every evening, except for Fridays, when there's fish.

—I just thought you wanted fish, is all she has to say on the matter.

Every now and then, I call Dad when I come out of the restaurant, although not a lot lately. He's normally doing his own cooking at around that time, which means that the calls generally revolve around whether I can help him to decipher Mom's recipe notes. The next time I call him he tells me that Jósef is coming for dinner so he thought of inviting Bogga as well. She's invited him three times, once for lamb soup, then fish in breadcrumbs, and glazed ham, so now he feels the need to return the favor and invite her over to his place, and he needs some advice:

—Do you remember any of Mom's ball recipes?

—Meat or fish balls?

—Fish. I've tried frying a few but they all fall apart.

—Don't you need potato flour?

—With the balls, you mean? Mixed into the minced fish?

—Yeah, about two spoonfuls.

—Was there anything else that's supposed to go into it, Lobbi?

—Egg and onion, if I remember correctly.

—I knew I was doing something wrong.

He's silent a moment and then asks me if I've gotten to know any of the locals yet.

—No, just the priest really, Father Thomas.

—Are there no females winking at you there?

—No, nothing like that.

—What about Anna?

—There's nothing between us. These things just happen, Dad.

—I wouldn't let a chance like that go by if I were in your shoes.

—It's not as if I have any choice. Besides, it takes two. You can't just fall in love at the drop of a hat.

—It's a piece of cake, Dabbi lad.

I switch subject and tell him I've started to learn the language.

—Well, you've never had any problems with languages, Lobbi. Although it mightn't be such a great investment to learn a language that so few people speak, when there's already so very few people that speak your own language.

Then he adds that he recently heard that every week there's one language that dies in the world.

—Well I suppose I better go home and learn some grammar, I say to wind up the call.

—Are you sure you're not wasting your time learning a language that's threatened with extinction?

When I get back to the guesthouse I meet Father Thomas in the hall.

—You're welcome to come over for nostalgia.

—What do you mean?

—To watch *Nostalgia* with me. You have to be able to look suffering in the eye to be able to empathize with those who suffer.

Thirty-eight

The movies in the evening make a big difference, even though they're not subtitled and are in different languages. I even occasionally try to converse in the village vernacular with my neighbor from room number seven at a very rudimentary level. I sit there with a dictionary on my knees, which makes the conversations a bit slow but not impossible.

—There's everything in here but violence, my neighbor tells me. It's clear that on every film evening my host is renewing his acquaintance with some old masterpiece.

—I generally look at movies that are larger than life, he says, handing me a video case to look at. There's a great deal of both intelligence and longing in this film. He takes the tape from me and replaces it on the shelf. Then he grabs a bottle and closes the blinds.

—The claim that art has to represent reality is a strange one, he says out the window. You'd think people would have had enough of mundane reality.

When the film is in a language I don't understand, Father Thomas gives me the gist of the story in a few concise sentences. But even though he sometimes pauses the film twice or three times to bring me up to speed on what's happening, it's often difficult to figure out from his summaries what the film is actually about. His focus is more on trying to convey the creative spirit behind each director. He doesn't just restrict himself to the plot, but instead emphasizes the construction of certain images, pondering on camera angles, talking about the settings, and freezing the tapes to point out any unusual editing, which is his main field of interest in filmmaking.

—Beauty is in the eyes of the beholder, he says.

He's also interested in the psychological buildup, but he normally goes so far in his analyses that it's hard to keep up with him. More appropriately, he gives me some kind of guideline or key that I can use to decipher the meaning myself. Even though it's difficult to understand everything that's happening on the little screen, it's better than hanging around in my room alone every night. Father Thomas also has special theme weeks, which he dedicates to particular directors, subjects, or actors. At the end of them we have brief discussions about the content while we finish our drinks.

This evening's film is all in blues that don't come over too well on the old TV set, even though Father Thomas has drawn the blinds. The picture starts with a fatal accident on a rainy highway and ends with an ode to love by Saint Paul the Apostle, sung by a soprano. The heroine is surrounded by death throughout the film, but in the end she longs to live, even though she's lost everything worth living for. Before I even know it, I've mentioned my worries about death to Father Thomas.

—I'm not worried about death itself, I tell him, but rather I'm worried about my thoughts about death.

He's standing and drawing the blinds open; outside the sky is black.

—What do you mean when you say you constantly think about death?

—About seven to eleven times a day, depending on the day. Mostly early in the morning when I've just got into the garden and late at night in bed.

I'm half expecting him to ask me how often I think about the body and sex. I could even envisage discussing those things with him, but it's easier to start discussions about important things on a more manageable subject than sex. But if he were to ask me, I'd say about as often as death. Seven to eleven times a day. As the day progresses, thoughts about death start to give way to thoughts about the body, I would say.

If he had asked about plants the answer would have been similar, too. I think about plants as much as I think about sex and death. But instead he asks:

—How old are you?

—Twenty-two.

—And are you expecting a call from the Grim Reaper then?

God only knows what's going through his mind. He grabs the bottle and pours some kind of transparent liqueur into two glasses.

—Pear aquavit, he says. Then he continues: Few people give themselves enough time to think about death. Then there are also those who don't even have any time to die. A growing number of people. You're obviously a mature young man.

—I hope I can die more experienced, after having found myself.

—People spend their entire lives looking for themselves. You'll never reach any final conclusions on that front. You don't strike me as someone who's on his last legs.

He smiles.

—Well, obviously you've got to die sometime, I say, most people seem to die either too late or too soon, no one at the right time.

—Yes, that's true, we all die, but no one knows when or how, says the priest, finishing his glass in one slug. We're given a time, some are warned long in advance, others at very short notice. Then we reach the point when our lives are counted in quarters of an hour and finally minutes. We're all on the same boat when it comes to that.

There's a fly buzzing around the room; I can hear it more than see it. Father Thomas stands up, walks over to the open window, and the buzz stops.

—Did you kill it?

—No, I put it outside, says my spiritual father.

—Then it's just a short while until we die in the memory of those who survive us, I say.

—That's not always the case; think of Goethe. Father Thomas refills the glasses.

—Yeah, but for those of us who aren't Goethe.

—You're obviously a soulful and compassionate young man. He pats my shoulder, puts down the bottle, and sits down again. He's silent a moment.

—You're not suffering from heartbreak?

The question catches me off guard.

—No, but I do have a child. It's then that you realize you're mortal.

—I see.

A long silence descends on the room again. There's no way of knowing what the man of God is thinking.

—I'm trying to cut down on drinking, he says finally. I haven't started to drink on my own yet, though, so I probably don't need to be worried.

He's standing again, which means our get-together is over. I'm not a man for long conversations either.

—Tomorrow we'll take a look at *The Seventh Seal*, he says, so that we continue on the theme of death.

✳

Thirty-nine

After two weeks I've discovered a small bookshop down an alley off the main street, a few yards away from the guesthouse. I'm mainly looking for reading material on this peculiar local dialect, but I also find a postcard of the main church that Jósef might like to have. I glance at a few books lying on the table, open one or two, and browse through a few pages. It's then that I spot a violet cover with a pink flower on it; the peculiar shape of the crown is reminiscent of Mom's eight-petaled rose. When I open the book there are no pictures inside, just text.

—Gardening? I ask a girl who is pottering around the shop and keeping an eye on me. She might be the daughter of the owner who is sitting by the till; they have similar profiles.

—No, a novel, she says, blushing. This is the first local female in my age group that I've had any personal interaction with.

I've been pondering on ways of getting to know the villagers and learning their dying dialect, although the problem, of course, lies in the fact that I work alone and in silence in the garden and there are therefore no opportunities to practice the language.

Should I put up an ad in the bookshop asking for private lessons in this endangered language? Maybe the owner's daughter would tell me straight away, before she'd even pinned up the notice, that she could take on the task herself on Wednesdays after work.

—We close at six then, instead of eight.

✳

Forty

Although I'd rather work in the garden every day, Father Thomas insists I take Sundays off, so I need to find something to keep me occupied. By now I've restored the rose beds to their original layout, realigned the colors, trimmed the hedges and bushes on the sides of the old path, cleaned out the pond in the middle of the garden, and tied down most of the ivy rosebushes that are allowed to stay on the northern side of the monastery. Once I've finished planning the following week's work, I read books I borrow from the monks' library. On Sundays, Father Thomas watches a film in the afternoon, which means that I have to spend the evening on my own.

I can't really say with a good conscience that I'm lonely, although I do occasionally feel a longing under my quilt, or sheets and blankets rather, to have someone to go home with. I sometimes find it difficult to fall asleep; I feel there's something missing from the day and I don't want it to end immediately—just as difficult as I imagine it would to break off a relationship with someone. Although I think of my daughter every now and then and sometimes of her mother, too, mainly because they normally go together, the child in her mother's arms, I can't really say that I actually miss anyone from home. My daughter is still too small to feel any need for me.

I'm still the foreigner; nevertheless I'm starting to notice the life around me. The sounds of the village are gradually filtering through to me, and my world and the world of others are no longer two totally separate entities.

A number of villagers have started to greet me on the street. On top of my list, apart from Father Thomas, whom I meet every day, there's the girl in the bookshop. I've also started to understand the lingo a bit. After two weeks, there are maybe ten words I've heard more than once and understand; after three weeks, twenty stand out, crystal clear, like knobs of harder rock on a weathered surface. Then I try to coordinate the tenses of my verbs and make myself understood and feel that I'm making some progress. When I ask for thirteen postcards of the church, because I'm practicing my numbers, the girl in the bookshop bursts out laughing. Meanwhile her father sits at the till going over his accounts on a squared sheet of paper. As she's getting the postcards she asks me a question that's been puzzling her: am I the guy in the monastery garden? Several other people have asked me what I'm doing in this forsaken place. Then she turns to her dad, nods at him, and says a few words I don't understand. But I sense they're confirming their suspicion because they're both looking at me and nodding at each other.

I memorize their words and look them up in my dictionary when I get home.

—It's the rose boy, she says, counting the postcards. Then she puts them in a brown paper bag, which she folds at the top and hands to me.

Forty-one

Having discussed death with Father Thomas and now watched thirty-three film gems with him, as my host points out, while the credits roll over Andrei Rublev, I feel ready to take this to the next level and tell him about my obsession with the body and sex. It's not as if I'm confessing my sins, though, or anything like that, or that I'm looking for absolution, nor am I exactly looking for advice from a man who's used to hearing everything under the sun. I feel much more like I'm just trying to get some things off my chest with my neighbor and friend from the next room. I wish I'd been better prepared, though, or even made notes, instead of hurling myself straight into the glacial pool like this.

—Ever since I woke up after my appendix operation, I've been very preoccupied with the body, a lot more than before.

Father Thomas stretches toward the bottle.

—And by body you mean…?

—Thoughts about sex, I say.

—It's not unnatural to be preoccupied with the body at your age.

—I don't think about the body all the time, but I do think about these things a lot, at least several hours a day.

—I don't think that's far from the average.

When I'm out on the street I mainly see other people as bodies. I don't even notice what they're saying to me. Although I wouldn't say that specifically applies to Father Thomas. He fills the glasses. The contents are bloodred today.

—Sometimes I feel I'm just a body, or at any rate that ninety-five percent of me is a body, I say.

—Cherry liqueur, he says. He concentrates on pouring into the glasses; then he seems to glance at a video case lying on the table. I have a feeling he's going to recommend a film to me.

—The problem is, I say, that my body seems to lead an independent existence with thoughts of its own. Otherwise I'm a normal young man.

Father Thomas studies me for a moment. Then he stands up, rearranges a few things on the desk, repositions the pen stand, places the Bible right in the middle of the desk, and puts two movies back in their places on the shelf.

—A man is both spirit and flesh, he says finally. I wouldn't be worried about it if I were you. He moves the pen stand back to its original position on the desk and then adds: Of course, it's a bit tedious for a twenty-two-year-old man to be glued to films every night with a forty-nine-year-old priest. Don't you think it would be good for you to go out and meet young people of your own age and blend in with the villagers?

I'm not exactly tired so I go out for some fresh air. On my way I meet a scraggy cat wandering alone but refrain from patting it. Before I know it, I'm standing in the phone booth and pumping it with coins. I get the feeling I'm the only person who uses this phone in the village. Dad kicks off the conversation by telling me that Bogga's cat, which had vanished for three days, has been found dead. Someone ran over him and left him on the flower bed. He also has a question for me.

—Who is Jennifer Connelly?

—I've never heard of her. Why do you ask?

—Because she's coming to the country this weekend.

—Says who?

—It was in the paper. On the front page.

—I don't know her.

—Do you need any cash, Lobbi?

—No, I'm fine. You can't spend any money here, apart from the coins that go into this phone.

I realize in mid call that there's a dead dove lying on the path right beside the phone booth. Part of one of its wings seems to be missing; I immediately suspect the cat. I've always had an aversion to dead or wounded animals, particularly feathered ones. When I step out of the phone booth I realize the bird isn't dead, the wing stump is moving. I pick up the wounded bird without knowing what I'm supposed to do with it. After walking with it for a few yards, its heart stops beating in the palm of my hand.

Forty-two

As I'm about to set off for the garden the following morning, Father Thomas knocks on my door to say he has some results on the matter.

—The body is discussed in one hundred and fifty-two places in the Bible, death in one hundred and forty-nine, and roses and other forms of plants in two hundred and nineteen instances. I counted them for you. Plants took the longest; there are fig trees and grapevines hidden all over the place. The same applies to fruit and all the types of seeds.

He hands me a semi-crumpled sheet of squared paper with three columns of figures, and points at the totals he has double underlined at the bottom of each one, to corroborate his words; these three figures say everything that needs to be known about what lies in my heart.

—There you have it in black and white, he says. The body, death, and roses, as if he were presenting some old pulp fiction paperback to me.

—You should look into it when you get a chance, he adds. The sheet only contains a load of numbers that have been written with a blunted pencil, no scriptural references or page numbers.

Then he says:

—Let's have an espresso and a bun before you go off to the garden.

As we're heading toward the café, Father Thomas suddenly remembers something else.

—There's also a letter to you, he says, pulling an envelope out of his pocket and handing it to me. It's not Dad's handwriting, although I wouldn't put it past him to send me a whole handwritten speech by post, on top of our conversations on the phone. Father Thomas points at the stamp and asks me about the bird.

—A snow bunting, I say.

The letter is from Anna, one-and-a-half pages written in big letters. I race over the pages and then read them again carefully. She gives me the latest news on my daughter, who's growing well, has six teeth and two more on the way. *She's a wonderful girl and such a luminous child, a real light,* she writes. She winds off by asking me to ring her as soon as possible and includes a phone number. I needn't be worried, though, she says, it's just something she wants to ask me about. Attached to the letter are two new photographs of Flóra Sól, about nine months old. She is in blue, padded overalls with a white hood, and stares at the photographer with big bright eyes. I glance at the postmark; the letter was posted eight days ago. I last saw my child and her mother two months ago when I was saying good-bye to them.

—Is everything OK back home? Father Thomas asks.

I glance at the clock. It's a quarter to eight, a bit early to call home. I'll wait till the afternoon when I'm finished in the garden.

Forty-three

I feel uneasy and also sense some insecurity in the voice of my daughter's mother. She says she's going to go abroad to take a postgrad in human genetics, but she has to finish her thesis first, after which she has to go to the college for an interview and find some accommodation for herself and the child.

She was wondering, she says—and her voice suddenly grows so faint that I think I'm about to lose the connection—if I could be with Flóra Sól while she's finishing her thesis and preparing herself. It might be for like a month, she says in an almost tapering voice.

—She's a very sweet and easygoing child, I hear her say.

Her request throws me completely.

—I also think it's good for you two to get to know each other, Anna continues. After all, she's your daughter, too, and you have to bear your part of the responsibility.

She's right, I was partly responsible for the conception of the child. I've replayed that scene in the greenhouse hundreds of times in my head and think it must have been some stranger, some other man that must have done the deed.

—I can't come home, I say, I'm stuck here with at least another month's work.

—I know, she says quickly, I'd bring Flóra Sól over to you. Your dad tells me that you can pretty much set your own timetable, that you're learning some rare dialect and thinking things over.

So that's what Dad is saying, that I'm thinking things over. My gardening doesn't even come into the equation.

I try one last card:

—The place isn't exactly on the beaten track and it's quite complicated to get here. I don't think it's a very suitable journey for an eight-month-old child.

—Almost nine months now, says Anna.

—Yeah, for an almost nine-month-old child, I say. After the flight, you've got to change trains four times and then take a bus from the next town because there are no trains here. There are two buses a day.

—I know, she says in a low voice, I've looked it up on the map. Flóra Sól won't be a problem, she's a very manageable child, as you'll get to realize. It's no bother traveling with her, she eats when she's hungry, sleeps when she's tired, and always wakes up happy. She also likes observing people and following what's going on around her. She's never been abroad, says Anna, as if this were a vital ingredient for the development of a nine-month-old child.

I somehow get the feeling that the decision has already been made, that the mother of my child will come with my roughly nine-month-old Flóra Sól and that I won't be given any chance to think the matter over. She's obviously thought this over inside out; Dad must have surely given her his backing in the decision and encouraged her. I wouldn't be surprised if he'd even planted the idea in her himself. I can almost hear him say it:

—Sure, it's a piece of cake, Dabbi.

Just as my life is starting to flow effortlessly, the garden having undergone a great transformation, and I am beginning to be able to exhale simple phrases in a new language, this has to happen. There are only two options for me: to say yes or no. I've never been any good at final or categorical decisions that rule out any other possibilities. Or at least not when there are people and feelings involved.

—Could you think about it and give me a call tomorrow? she asks. I sense her unease; she seems to be worried, as if she were already starting to wish she hadn't called me. I don't feel particularly good myself. That's women for you. They're suddenly there in front of you, on the threshold of a new life with a child in their arms, telling you that you've got to bear responsibility for a poorly timed conception, an accidental child.

—I'll pick you up at the station, I say as if someone else is speaking through me, it's too complicated getting here by bus.

There's silence on the line, as if my response had somehow thrown her.

—Don't you want to think it over and call me tomorrow?

—No, there's no need, I say and feel how unlike myself I am. Without having any idea of what role Anna has just cast me in or what taking care of the child entails, I don't want to disappoint the mother of my child or let my daughter down. It's only fair that I should share responsibility for the child with her mother. I was even present at her birth, although it would be too far-fetched to say that I delivered her or that I was of any use.

—Thank you for taking it so well; to be honest, I didn't know what to expect. I had no other choice, she says finally, almost in a whisper, as if she had written me the letter as a last resort.

—There's just one other thing: I'll bring everything but a bed; do you think you could get a cot for Flóra Sól? Just for a while, it can be secondhand.

❁

Forty-four

After my conversation with Anna I knock on Father Thomas's door. He's started to watch the movie without me, because I was late, and pulls a chair out for me. I get straight to the point.

—Something's come up, I say. The thing is, I have to take care of a child, my nine-month-old daughter, in fact, just for a while, probably for three or four weeks. Could she stay with me in the guesthouse and be with me in the garden during the day? I'd probably have to reduce my workload a bit.

Father Thomas turns off the TV and stares at me in disbelief, as if he were wondering if he'd heard me right.

—I'd find a bed for her, I say; it would only be temporary, I add.

There is a prolonged silence in room number seven. Father Thomas finally speaks.

—There is no space for a child within the framework of monastic life. It would disturb the tranquility and prayers.

—I wouldn't exactly be taking her into the monastery, I say, just to the garden. Her mother says she sleeps three hours after lunch, so she could sleep in the carriage while I work in the rose garden.

—No, no, and no. The child would disrupt everything. When a baby babbles, it can be heard. What do you think Brother Jacob would say?

—It would only be temporary, I say, starting to repeat myself and sensing that my arguments bear little weight. I don't know why he specifically mentioned Brother Jacob.

—Are you going to take a babbling child to the refectory? For soup and a jar full of baby food? He looks at me with a mixture of horror and amazement. This isn't a hotel, it's a monastery. The men who are here have renounced family life to serve God. Are you going to set up a nursery in that world? Only Christ comes first in here.

—But didn't Christ say come all you…, I hazard feebly, but immediately sense my sarcasm is out of place. I feel like I'm rapidly losing ground.

—Christ said and Christ didn't say, are you so infantile as to think you can argue theology with me?

—There now, he says in a milder tone. Let's have a drop of apricot liqueur.

He grabs a bottle and glasses.

—You never mentioned you had a child. Just that your mother had died and that you were pondering about death and the body.

—One can't always cover everything. I thought I'd told you about it, though, when we were discussing death.

—It isn't always easy to know what you're getting at.

Although the matter is formally closed, I attempt to play my final trump card by showing Father Thomas a photograph of my daughter. I choose the older picture, the one of her straight out of the tub in her bath gown, because I think it'll have the greatest impact. She has a cordon tied around her waist like a monk and wet curly locks on her forehead. The bare toes that protrude from the hem of the gown are the size of peas.

He examines the photograph, impossible to decipher what he's thinking.

—To be honest, I thought you weren't interested in women. It even occurred to me that you might have a crush on me, he says with a smile. I'm relieved that's not the case. I was going to shake you off, but I don't have to now, says the priest, leaning back on his chair. The matter is settled, as far as he is concerned. He tells me I'm welcome to stay on and watch the rest of the film with him; he can fill me in on the story so far, the first twenty minutes. The theme is faith this time for a change, a quarter-of-a-century-old picture by Godard.

—We don't just have a need to know everything, but also to believe, says the priest, setting the tone for the content of this masterpiece. If a girl who is expecting a child says she hasn't slept with anyone, it may well be true. It is by no means necessary to see to believe. Unless she defines the act differently. And the word became flesh, as the text says. Thus every woman carries the mystery of genesis within her, the light of divine conception.

I slip my daughter's photograph back into my pocket. There is little else to add. I watch the film distractedly for half an hour, then stand up and say good night.

—Don't worry, you'll find a solution to your problem with God's help, he says, the Lord be with you and your child.

Forty-five

The girls are arriving in five days. Why did I agree to take the child, what on earth was I thinking? Here I am in a dream garden where literally everything I plant in the earth grows, and my life is taking on some shape. Although I'm a father I've no idea of what's best for a child; I don't even know what's best for me. You could say that I ended up having a child before I even got a chance to figure out if I wanted one or not.

I decide to go to the garden later than usual today and to have a haircut instead, while I try to rethink my life from scratch. It says barber on the sign, but it also seems to be a hair salon for ladies, with three archaic hair dryers. The woman in the salon washes my hair. She takes a long time to spread the shampoo and very slowly massages me around the ears and all around my scalp. She has black hair and tells me that there are two of them working there in shifts. Then she says I have thick hair and that she's spotted me a few times on the street and looked at my hair. Finally, she asks me how short I want it to be. Meanwhile I'm thinking of Anna, whom I only saw for ten minutes about two months ago when I was saying good-bye to her in the hall, and before that, but only kind of, in the maternity ward. That isn't altogether true either, because I popped in to see the child between my trips out at sea; the last time I brought a doll and tomatoes.

And yet, to be honest, I wouldn't be able to describe the mother of my child in any way that would enable a stranger to recognize her from my description, let's say to the police, for example, if something came up and the girls didn't get off the train.

—What kind of a nose does she have?

—I'm not sure. Feminine.

—Can you describe her in detail?

—Not much.

—And her mouth?

—Average size.

—What do you mean by average size? What kind of lips does she have?

—Thick, I think. Should I say a cherry mouth? I try to remember her sleeping face in the maternity ward.

—Color of her eyes?

—Not sure, blue or green.

Instead I try to conjure up that private memory, the light in the greenhouse and her leaf-patterned body.

I feel the need to rehearse the new situation that has unexpectedly cropped up in my life so I tell the woman that I'm expecting my daughter, about nine months old, and her mother on a visit. The woman nods, full of understanding. I immediately regret divulging this unnecessary information, which could just as easily have been left at the bottom of the ocean as far as I was concerned.

I stand out in the sun in the square with my newly cut hair while it dries and also to give myself time to recover from the emotion. People are staring at me; maybe they're unused to seeing men with wet hair on the street. In just a few days' time, I'll no longer be the rose boy but the foreigner with the baby carriage.

When I get back to the guesthouse that evening after working in the garden, Father Thomas is waiting for me in the hall. Do you need an apartment for you and the child? he asks without hesitation.

—I've spoken to a nice woman and put in a good word for you. She can give you a apartment just here on the next street, he says.

—It's only temporary, I say.

—Yeah, exactly, temporary, that's what I told her. How long did you say the child would be staying for, four weeks?

—Yeah, at the most.

—It's furnished. It's normally empty, you just have to pay for the gas and cover a few minor expenses.

—I can take a look at the apartment tomorrow.

After I've thanked him, Father Thomas has something else he needs to get off his chest. He tells me that the monks are very happy with everything I've done with the roses so far; they also fully understand the temporary changes in my situation and hope to get me back when my circumstances permit.

—You can come to the garden if you find someone to baby-sit the child. Weren't you saying that the little one takes a snooze in the afternoon? Brother Martin, broadly speaking, approves of the ivy plants but shares the same concerns that Brother Jacob has, that it might carry bugs into the building. He asks me to remind you that his room is on the southern side, the same side as Brother Stephen's room, who is allergic to pollen.

Forty-six

My first home after Dad's house is on the second floor of a building with a mint-green facade. The apartment stretches lengthwise and is made up of two rooms that lead into each other with incredibly high ceilings that are totally out of sync with the small size of the apartment.

—Twenty feet, says the woman when I look up at the ceiling, indicating six with her fingers. The bedroom, which is accessed through the dining room, has a double carved bed and wallpaper with a white fleur-de-lis pattern against a maroon background, and an antique-looking painting hangs over the bed.

—The flight from Egypt, the woman explains somewhat at length. The furniture could be collector's items from an old manor. The apartment is nevertheless clean and bright and there are no personal effects, apart from two painted plaster statues standing on the chest of drawers in the bedroom: a stooping old man with a halo and a monk in a habit with a child in his arms, also with a halo.

—Saint Joseph and Saint Anthony of Padua, the woman explains to me. She tells me that the apartment belongs to her sister, who has moved out with most of her personal belongings, so it's therefore almost completely empty.

The other room is bigger and some kind of sitting room, dining room, and kitchen all rolled into one. There's a sofa you can pull out and use as a sofa bed, says the woman.

—If need be, she adds looking at me from head to toe, as if she were surprised that the priest should have taken me under his wing.

The rent is practically nothing. I think the woman might have even made a mistake; I actually only pay for the gas.

—Gas is extra, she says.

There are mirrors literally everywhere; I count seven of them in total, which makes the place look bigger and almost gives it the semblance of a maze. For a moment it feels like there are three women standing close to me. Although I have no experience of a nine-month-old child, it occurs to me that she might find mirrors fun.

—This is only temporary, I say.

—So Father Thomas was saying. He said it would be six weeks to begin with and that you'll be having a little child with you.

She studies me carefully; maybe she thinks I don't look much like a father?

I suddenly look into the mirror beside me and meet the worried gaze of a man with newly cut red hair. Although it could, of course, be a good antidote to loneliness, there is something peculiar about being mirrored all the time, about being constantly reminded of one's self.

The woman says she is going to lend me some bedclothes. I'm not sure I fully understood whether she is coming back with them straight away or later, but meanwhile I don't dare leave the building.

After the woman has left, I lie on the bed and discover on the bedroom ceiling, twenty feet above, the remnants of a fresco depicting winged angels spiraling around a blue hole in the celestial vault. In the middle of the blue sky there is a white dove with a wing missing. I stand up and take another round of the apartment. On the desk there is a vase with plastic flowers; to me a home can never be a home unless there are living flowers, so I take the vase and stick it into an empty kitchen cupboard.

—Where are the flowers? is the first question the woman asks me when she returns with a pile of ironed bedclothes in her arm.

I walk over to the cupboard, open it, and hand her the vase with the plastic flowers without saying a word. She takes it and puts it back on the table again, in the exact same spot as before. When the woman is gone and I'm left standing alone on the threshold of my first apartment with three keys in my hand, I put the plastic decoration back into the cupboard again. Then I draw back the thick curtains in the bedroom. They're made of red velvet with interwoven patterns that look like fire lilies, with double silk lining; I have the feeling they might have been moved from a grander house. It makes sense; turning them, you can see that the hem has been shortened and re-sewn. The windows extend to the floor and open onto a balcony with a railing; I estimate it can hold a stool and four or five potted plants.

Forty-seven

Unusually, the theme of the week at my guesthouse neighbor's film club is the early movies of forgotten Hollywood stars. I decide to skip the film that shot Jane Wyman into stardom and instead scrub the apartment. I feel the need to clean up before the girls arrive, so I pop into the shop to buy a detergent with a lemon smell. This is my first purchase in the village, apart from books and postcards.

The child has to be able to crawl on the floor in her light yellow leggings. My nine-month-old daughter must be crawling by now, right? It occurs to me that I should have asked Anna if the child has started to crawl yet. While the water is heating on the gas cooker, I walk around the apartment and wonder if it's homey enough. I can think of nothing better than filling it with plants. I'm not familiar enough with the shops so it takes me some time to find some clay pots for them. Finally I come home with carnations, hydrangea, lilies, and a rose I picked from the garden, and also rosemary, thyme, basil, and mint, and place the pots on the edge of the balcony.

I then need to buy other necessities for the new home. Some questions remain unanswered. The train is arriving in the afternoon. Will the mother of my child hand me the child at the station and take the next train back, or will she come up to the village to check out the state of the apartment? Will she even be staying for dinner? If so, should it be a formal dinner with us sitting around a table? I've been in the village for two months now and haven't cooked a single meal yet. I decide to be prepared for the unexpected and assume the mother of my child will be staying for dinner. For safety I also assume that she will stay one night on the sofa bed and catch the train the day after. Although I've been pretending to help Dad to remember how Mom cooked things over the phone, my knowledge of cooking is pretty limited. I never cooked at home, although I sometimes used to hang over Mom in the kitchen. My baptism of fire in gastronomy happened at sea on those few occasions when we couldn't drag the cook out of bed. I was taken out of the fish slime and transferred to the kitchen, where the Latin genius found himself trying to fry greasy meatballs and pork chops in bread crumbs with sweet-and-sour sauce for the crew—I'm incapable of cooking anything. The pork chops came preprepared in the breadcrumbs and the sweet-and-sour sauce from a bottle; all I had to do was pour the contents of the bottle into the pan. Then I fried some eggs with it, a personal added touch that went down well, so there weren't that many complaints. I also fried eggs for my brother Jósef when he was hungry; he isn't critical by nature and never questions anything I do. That sums up my knowledge of cooking.

What does an approximately nine-month-old eat? Presuming my daughter has two teeth on her upper gum and four teeth below, does that mean she can eat meat mashed in a sauce or only mashed baby food? I try to recall the things I might be able to cook without much bother. It occurs to me that I could handle making meatballs in brown sauce if I can find the basic ingredients.

Forty-eight

I work until after dark on the days leading up to the girls' arrival, but on the last morning I search the village from a new perspective: food shops. I'm quick to work my way through the streets where most of the necessities are to be found. Bread can be bought next door to the meat, and vegetables and fruit, seeds, beans, jam, and coffee are in the shop opposite. Sausage and olives and all kinds of pickles are behind a glass display at the butcher's. In the square in front of the church they sell cheeses, raw ham, and bee honey. I start at the butcher's but can't see any minced meat anywhere. Instead I point at the light red pieces of meat on display.

—That's veal, says the butcher. I'm almost relieved it's not pork and think of Dad.

—Yes, exactly, I'll have two pounds, I say without hesitation.

The butcher whips the lump of meat up on the carving board and cuts eight slices with a razor-sharp knife, sliding it smoothly through the bloody muscles, observing me as he does so. Next I dare to point at a bowl with some marinated delicacy in it that looks interesting to me.

—A quarter pound, I say in flawless dialect, because the woman before me asked for a quarter pound, too.

—A quarter pound? the butcher asks, raising an eyebrow. I get the feeling the other three customers are staring at me as well. He then fishes out the marinated artichokes with a sieve spoon, places them on thick wax paper and at lightning speed folds the paper at the ends and throws it on the scales.

When I come home with bags of food in my arms, Brother Marcus and Brother Paul are already far up the stairs carrying a small white cot. They're turning on the landing of the second floor and seem relieved to see me. The neighbors on the top and ground floors have stepped out to watch these two movers in white hooded habits.

—We've brought you the bed, they say. Where would you like it?

I've no recollection of telling Father Thomas that I needed a bed for the child. I put down the bags and, once I've found the right key to open the apartment, help them with the cot, which we put down in the bedroom. Once Brother Marcus and Brother Paul have left again, after turning down my offer of some teabag tea, I empty the bags and arrange the shopping on the kitchen table. Two pounds of potatoes, eight flattened slices of veal, a quarter pound of marinated artichokes, a bottle of water, milk, olive oil, a jar of honey, cheese, salt, and a pepper pot.

The girls are arriving in the afternoon, and on my last trip to the garden in the morning I picked a bundle of roses that I place in the vase that held the plastic flowers. Then I knock on my neighbor's door on the top floor, an old woman with silvery hair, to borrow an iron from her. She's slightly bewildered but lends it to me anyway. I iron the only shirt I brought from home, which is the same shirt I was in when my daughter Flóra Sól was born.

The mother and daughter are arriving at five and I'm standing there, clueless it must be said, in front of the meat I've just bought. In the end I go back to the butcher and ask him how I'm supposed to cook the meat I bought from him half an hour ago. I'm wearing the white shirt.

My question doesn't seem to surprise him in the least.

—Wasn't it veal?

—Yeah, that's right. Two pounds.

—Yeah, eight slices, should be enough for five adults, he says.

—Yes, there were eight slices, I say. I've made some progress in the language; I can form short simple sentences and hold a conversation.

—You heat the pan, he says, then put four tablespoons of oil in it and fry the slices of meat in the oil, first on one side and then you turn them over and fry them on the other side. Then just salt and pepper. It doesn't take long.

—How long? I ask.

—Three minutes on each side.

—What about a sauce? I ask.

—You pour red wine over the pan when you've finished frying the meat and let the sauce sizzle a moment.

—How long?

—Two minutes.

—And spices?

—Salt and pepper.

※

Forty-nine

She's holding my daughter in her arms when she steps off the train, and there aren't many people on the platform so they stand out in the crowd and attract plenty of attention. Flóra Sól is in a pink floral dress, stockings, pink shoes, and a knitted sweater. She's grown; she's no longer an infant. She's wearing a yellow hat that is knotted under her chin, and two golden locks protrude from the rim over her forehead. I stare at the child, the fruit of a fleeting moment of carnal pleasure, whom I haven't seen for two months, and she stares back at me with big, watery blue eyes, curious and slightly hesitant. Anna is wearing a blue jacket with her hair tied in a tail, and is visibly tired after the journey. I also get the feeling that she might be cold, even though it's hot out and I'm wearing a shirt myself.

The first thought that crosses my mind when I see her getting off the train is that I should have made an effort to get to know her better. Three years ago I wouldn't have noticed a girl like her on the street; it would be different today, though, because I'm not the same man anymore. They're both eyeing me up, the mother and daughter: I'm in a freshly ironed shirt and have a new haircut, that's the best I could do.

I greet Anna with a kiss on the cheek and smile at my daughter. She smiles back with a wet smile, rosy cheeks, and dimples on her pale porcelain face; there is a great brightness around the child. My daughter stretches out her hand toward me. Her mother looks at her in surprise and then at me, as if the child had somehow stunned her by immediately taking to her stranger of a father. She, nevertheless, hands me my daughter. She's as light as a feather, about the weight of a big puppy, and all soft. She leaps into my arms. I stroke her cheek.

—She's not afraid of strangers, her mother explains. She trusts people.

I should probably be asking myself how two virtual strangers could have conceived such a divine child in such a primitive and inappropriate setting as a greenhouse. I almost feel a pang of guilt. So many people play everything by the book, have exemplary courtships, gradually save up the things they'll need, found a relationship, become mature enough to handle disagreements and meet all their payment obligations, and yet still don't manage to create the child they have dreamed of.

It's a fifteen-minute drive from the train station to the village. The lemon-yellow car that has been sitting there motionless for about two months reached its destination without a hitch.

—It's incredibly beautiful here, the mother of my child says, as we approach the village. Although it's more remote than I imagined, she adds.

I explain to her that from this point onward, it's all uphill and that we have to walk.

—The apartment I'm renting is behind the church, I say, pointing up the hill toward the top of the village and my newly founded home. The monastery stretches out before us, but I decide this isn't the right moment to discuss the rose garden.

Anna has a fold-up stroller which we open and place the luggage in; then I grab a bottle of wine for the sauce from the box I got from the proprietor of the restaurant and stick an additional two into the rack under the stroller. I'd forgotten the wine, and I can give Father Thomas a bottle now. I hold my daughter in my arms as we walk up the hill, and she looks around with curiosity.

On the way I steal some glimpses of the girl walking beside me; she has a pretty profile.

—Have you heard anything from Thorlákur? I ask. Why on earth am I asking about him?

—No, I haven't heard from him since we did a runner on him at your birthday party a year and a half ago, she says with a laugh.

I'm relieved she laughed at my stupid question. She has aquamarine eyes, so I can add that detail to the personal description I needed. She also has a pretty smile; it isn't difficult to like her, and since I had to accidentally have a child I'm at least glad it was with her. It's only been thirty minutes since the girls stepped off the train, and that's all the reacquaintance I need to want to tell the mother of my child that I'm willing to be her friend and organize the child's birthdays with her, and even volunteer to come over just before Easter every year to trim the trees in her garden—I don't say in her and her husband's garden. Then I realize that this is neither the place nor the time for openness.

I don't ask her when she's taking the train back; instead I tell her I've cooked dinner, which is my way of telling her that she's invited to stay for dinner. I've already fried the veal and boiled the potatoes and only have to make the sauce now.

—This is quite an achievement, I say, I'm not exactly used to cooking. She smiles again, warmly.

The mother of my child looks somewhat taken aback when she enters the apartment.

—This is an incredible apartment, she says, like something out of an old fairy tale. She walks into the bedroom and runs her fingers against the fire lily wallpaper. And flowers everywhere, she says, when she sees the kitchen and I open the balcony door for her. I sense from her voice that she might be touched. As soon as mother and child step into my dwelling, my first attempt to create a home, it's as if everything grows brighter, as if the place is filled with light.

—Are you sure it's OK? she asks, gazing around her. It's impossible to tell what feelings she might be harboring.

I'm still holding the child in my arms; the lower half of her body is starting to slide. I imagine she might need a change of diaper pretty soon.

—Well, I found a cot, I say, loosening my daughter's hat. She's got some blonde hair now, mainly over the forehead where the curls are. I quickly glance in the mirror to look at us together, my daughter and me; she's full of miniature features and it's difficult to pinpoint any obvious resemblance. I stroke her head.

—She's got the exact same ears as you, says the budding geneticist, observing me.

She's right, my ears are shaped in the same mold, same folds, same kind of earlobes. I swiftly compare her to her mother with aquamarine eyes, but I don't spot any striking resemblance either, apart from the shape of the mouth, which is similar, two varieties of cherry mouths. But apart from the ears and cherry-shaped mouth, the person our daughter seems to resemble the most is herself, as if she were of some other origin. I sense Mom in her, though, is some undefined way, even though I can't quite put my finger on it, except her dimples maybe, although I wouldn't give Dad the satisfaction of pointing it out to him. And also there was always sunshine wherever Mom was, no matter what the weather was like outside. She was full of light somehow; in the photographs it always looked like she was lit up by a spotlight, and in group shots she was the only one with radiant cheeks. You'd almost think the pictures were overexposed. There was light in Mom's hair, like in this child's hair, like glitter sprinkled over it, and there was a luminosity in the smile. I fully admit that I'm sensitive about Mom; I was sensitive about her when she was alive and still am now. I was born pale with a few straws of red hair, and my twin brother with dark hair, dark skin, and brown eyes.

All of a sudden I feel a longing to show Anna a picture of Mom, but I know that this is hardly the right moment to be claiming a greater share in my child's genes, not now when she's about to say good-bye to the child and is no doubt feeling vulnerable.

—She's unusually easygoing and good, her mother says, always happy and in a good mood, wakes up with a smile and sleeps all night.

We walk out of the kitchen into the bedroom.

—Don't let her out of your sight for a second, she continues, she crawls around everywhere and is very curious, she might climb into a cupboard or crawl under the bed, or she might fiddle with sockets. Even though she's a precocious kid and more mature than other children of her age, she's still totally guileless.

—I've drawn up a list, she says, of the things you need to watch out for. She pulls out a folded sheet of paper. What she can eat and not.

—Are there things she can't eat?

—The food, of course, has to be very well mashed; she's got six teeth and there are two extra ones on the way.

Then she opens a changing bag, shows me what's in it, and lets me practice changing the baby. I place the child on the double bed.

—You don't have to take off her cardigan when you're changing her, says the mother, demonstrating.

I lift up the floral dress and pull off her stockings. Then I unfasten two poppers on some kind of bodysuit underwear. There's just the diaper left. My daughter smiles from ear to ear; then she splutters, and finally the sounds seem to change into syllables: *da da da da.*

—She's not saying *daddy*, she's practicing her consonants, Anna says abruptly, and I almost sense a crack in her voice. She's probably tired; the child, on the other hand, looks rested and happy.

I remove the diaper. No question about it, she's a girl.

—You don't have to powder or put cream on her every time, Anna explains. She stands beside me, watching me with an apprehensive air. I lift up the bodysuit slightly to see the bulge of her tummy, her navel gently protruding from the summit of the dome of her belly like a bell. She has a tiny birthmark on her groin in the exact same spot as me. So that's two traits she's inherited from her father's side: the earlobes and birthmark, three if we throw Mom's dimples into the equation. I can't stop myself from bending over and blowing lightly on her tummy. The child giggles. Then I stoop down slightly farther and kiss her stomach. The child smells good. I'm not sure how the woman who is watching me is taking this; she has an indecipherable look on her face, as if she were on the verge of tears.

—Do you have any experience with children? Anna asks. She looks at me as if she is starting to regret this whole affair.

—No, actually.

It's true, I don't feel I can mention the fact that I still hold my disabled twin brother's hand.

—But I feel OK about it, I add.

When I've finished changing my daughter, she holds out her hands and smiles at me. I smile back. Keeping her arms outstretched, she tenses her tummy. She's stopped smiling and has, in fact, started to whimper, although no tears are visible. Finally she turns over on her stomach and sits up by herself.

—She wants to be picked up, says my interpreter, the child's mother, as if she is somehow relieved. I bend over and lift the child off the bed.

Next she teaches me how to use the stroller. There are two positions, one so that she can sit up and look at people and her surroundings. In fact, Flóra Sól is very interested in people and her surroundings, says her mother. Then there's the other position: Like this, she says, pressing a button and pushing the bottom of the buggy up—then you have a carriage that Flóra Sól can sleep in. I nod; it seems pretty straightforward. I'm not sure I've got it all right, though, but I'm sure I'll figure it out, I can always practice the settings when the child is asleep.

—She has three pacifiers, says the mother. She hangs the pink changing bag on my shoulder to show me how to carry it around. Then she also needs to explain to me how it works. It's like a soft tool bag, with countless side pockets and compartments in which you can store spare diapers and stockings, and keep creams, extra pacifiers, and wipes, says Anna, except that you can also open it up on all sides and flatten it out so that it turns into a changing table. The child's mother has learned all these tricks and more in less than nine months. The future genetics expert's skills leave me in awe. How can a young woman, a biology student, change into a mother in such a short time?

—This will be for four weeks at the most, she says, but with an expression that seems to say there's no way she'll be able to handle it. All going well, three and a half.

—Don't worry, I say.

—Are you sure it'll be OK? she asks, although I've already twice confirmed, against my better judgment, that everything will be just fine. I lift her daughter up to show her how easy it'll be and how good I feel about being alone with the child for four weeks, and she giggles and laughs. Then she places her little palm on my face and pats my cheek; she's aware of her responsibility.

—She's very tender, always wants to pat people, her mother explains.

—Da-da, says my daughter and then lays her head on my shoulder, right under my cheek.

—I'll have loads of things to do with my thesis, then I've got to sort out accommodation and get the application forms for colleges. You can always call me, of course, she says, handing me a note with two telephone numbers on it. If I'm not there just leave a message. She's got that verging-on-tears look again.

Then I remember the meal that I've spent half the day preparing.

—I've cooked a meal, I say again, and I don't ask her what time her train is leaving.

—Thanks, she says, relieved.

It was a fair while ago, actually, so I need to heat up the meat and potatoes again and make some red wine sauce. I didn't think of asking the butcher about any side dishes, so I just boiled the potatoes, carrots, and cabbage together in one pot. I shift the vase with roses and lay three plates on the table, two side by side and one opposite. The girls are watching me. Anna takes out a cup with a lid and a spout for the child and places it beside one of the two plates that are beside each other.

—Flóra Sól can eat meat so long as it's minced into tiny pieces, she says.

My child's mother eats two helpings of food and praises it to the heavens. She's obviously hungry.

—This is really good, she says.

We drink whatever wine didn't go into the sauce. Dad made a dessert for me when I was leaving, but I haven't made any now.

—I'm taking the train tomorrow morning; is it OK if I stay tonight? Anna asks, averting her gaze. I can sleep on the sofa, she quickly adds, having checked the setup in the apartment.

I surrender my bed to the girls and pull out the sofa bed for myself. Anna puts the child to bed and dresses her in a night bodysuit with pictures of puppies on it. She rubs some cream into her daughter's cheeks, brushes her eight teeth, and combs the curls on her forehead back to one side with a wet, soft brush. Then she brings her over and gets her to kiss me good night. Flóra Sól sticks the pacifier in her mouth herself, and I see her resting her head on her mother's shoulder as they disappear into the bedroom.

I wash up and Anna reappears a short while later; she's tired and wants to doze off with the child.

—Thank you so much for the great meal, she says. And thanks for taking this thing with Flóra Sól so well. It really saves me.

Then she says good night.

—Good night.

—Good night.

It's weird to think of the mother and daughter in the next room; it's just like it was nine months ago in the maternity ward, we're all sleeping under the same roof again. I wonder whether it would be appropriate to go out in the evening, but don't feel like leaving Anna alone in the apartment with the child. There's no point in me groping around the rose garden in the pitch dark either. And even though I would undoubtedly be welcome to some black currant liqueur and a movie at Father Thomas's, I can see from the clock that I'd arrive in mid-film.

❋

Fifty

The following morning I wake up early. I bought everything we needed for dinner yesterday; now I need to buy breakfast. For the first time in two months I don't go to the garden.

I don't quite know what to buy, but come home with a packet of coffee, tea, bread, butter, bananas, cheese, and oatmeal. In the end, I also buy two buns. I bought the milk yesterday. By the time the girls come out, freshly woken and rosy cheeked, I've made porridge, something I learned from Dad, who always used to make porridge for Jósef and myself in the morning.

Anna is in a light blue T-shirt with an inscription on it and is wearing glasses and her hair in a tail. This is something I wouldn't have expected, for her to walk in like that in a light blue T-shirt with an inscription on the front, two words; my quick guess is that it's Finnish. She hands me our daughter. Flóra Sól is wearing a barrette at the top of her forehead.

All three of us sit at the breakfast table, like a family. I feed the child, who opens her mouth wide after each spoonful, like a hungry nestling. Then I peel a banana and hand it to her; she holds it with both hands and eats it without any assistance.

—Good girl, I say.

When she's finished eating the banana, she slaps her smudgy fingers on my face and I kiss them.

I sense Anna is feeling better than she did last night; she looks rested. Instead of looking apprehensive, she has a certain aloofness now, as if she isn't fully aware of me at the table.

—Is that Finnish? I ask, meaning her T-shirt.

—Yeah, life sciences conference, she says and smiles. Then she stands up and goes into the bedroom to pack her stuff.

—The train leaves at eleven, she says.

I'm sitting with my daughter in my arms.

When she comes back she hugs the child in her arms. The child smiles and says *ma ma*.

Anna doesn't want us to accompany her to the train station and says she'll take the bus. She might start crying, she says, by way of explanation. Although she's normally very gentle and reasonable, she can be pretty temperamental.

—I see, I say and my daughter presses her cheek against mine, running her fingers over my freshly shaved jaw.

—I'll be back in three to four weeks, one month altogether at the most, Anna says.

—Like I said, have no worries. Have a nice journey.

I don't want her to sense my insecurity.

She kisses the child. Then she kisses me on both cheeks. The child knows how to wave good-bye. Neither of them cry.

—I trust you, she says.

—Don't worry, I say, I'll take good care of her.

The child waves at her mom again.

I've just closed the door when there's a knock. I open it with Flóra Sól, my daughter, in my arms.

—I forgot something, says the girl standing at the door. She unzips her case and pulls out a package.

—It's from your dad. He sends all his love, of course. Sorry for being so absentminded.

She hands me the soft package that has been wrapped in Christmas gift paper and a green ribbon with frilly ends. It's the same kind of paper the pajamas were wrapped in.

I take the package and hand her daughter to her instead; we swap loads. She kisses her daughter on the cheek and hugs her as if after a long separation. Her case sits in the hall. I wonder if there's any way I can avoid opening the package in front of Anna, but the child is waiting in suspense; the two girls are staring at me waiting for me to open it, so I've got no choice. In the package there's a knitted blue sweater with a yellow and white patterned stripe running across it that would fit a two- or three-year-old. It reeks of washing powder. As explained in the accompanying letter from my father, it's my own sweater, *as you will have rightly surmised*, he says in the letter. *It was your mother who knit this sweater, one for each of you twins, actually, for your third birthday, and this one might have been worn by Jósef, since you were such a terrible messer and reduced almost all of your clothes to shreds, whereas your brother was* special *and didn't ruin anything, whether it was clothes, books, or toys,* he says in the handwritten letter. *Since you yourself have been blessed by the good fortune and miracle of having a wonderful child with a beautiful girl, hopefully this sweater will come in handy. Not only will this little family gift make your late mother very happy, but it will also build a bridge between generations and strengthen the child's bond with her father's side of the family, although perhaps more symbolically than anything else, not that I expect she'll have much use for it down there in those mild southern breezes blowing on those foreign shores, since it's also too big and the child is still small.* The letter ends with the wish that my daughter will grow up in this sweater that a good woman knitted for a three-year-old boy about nineteen years ago and that this will give her granddad on earth and granny in heaven boundless happiness and joy. The package also contains one of Mom's handwritten notebooks with her recipes.

I made a copy for myself, Dad writes, *but am giving you the original.* I open the worn-out copybook and quickly skim the pages, many of which are loose; they're mainly cookie recipes but I also spot cocoa soup with rusk and whipped cream.

—Your dad pops in to visit us sometimes, says the mother of my child, shuffling her feet at the door, he's quite a special man. Flóra Sól is very fond of him.

So Dad has been visiting his granddaughter and her mother again without telling me.

—We've also visited him a few times, says Anna, he showed me a photograph of you when you were five in Wellies and with freckles and also a class photo of you and exam results he kept. She seems to be genuinely fond of Dad.

—What is it he calls you again? He seems to use lots of nicknames. Lobbi, Addi, Dabbi?

—Yeah, that's right. He calls me Dabbi when he's about to discuss my future with me and what he thinks I should be doing.

She laughs, we both laugh. I'm relieved, so is she.

Then I say good-bye to Anna for the second time and wish her a nice journey and tell her once more not to have any worries. Being a man means being able to tell a woman not to have any worries.

I place my daughter on the double bed and open the bag that came with her and unpack it onto shelves in the wardrobe.

There are cotton bodysuits and stockings, lots of T-shirts, all kinds of soft pants with elastics around the waist and ankles, loads of incredibly small stockings, knitted sweaters, hats, two dresses, and the smallest anorak imaginable, all clean and neatly folded. There are a few toys, dolls, three rag animals, a jigsaw, and cubes with the letters of the alphabet. The child turns over on her tummy and jiggles toward the edge of the bed, legs first. She crawls backward like a lizard or jungle warrior at a training

camp. Her feet reach the edge of the bed. She carefully allows
herself to slide to the floor.

—Good girl, I say out loud.

She stands by the edge of the bed, smiling from ear to ear, on
her unsteady little legs, which she is beginning to learn how to
use, dimples under her chubby knees.

Even though I've washed everything with lemon detergent,
I'm not sure I want her crawling on the floor. The floor is cold and
I can't be sure she won't find something that she might want to
stick in her mouth.

—No, no, I say, don't crawl on the floor.

I pick her up and position her like a puppy on all fours on my
double bed.

—Crawl here, I say. I give clear messages, sentences limited
to two or, at the most, three words: subject, verb, object. And
then, almost in a whisper, I try out these new unfamiliar words
for my mouth, as if they are a new definition of myself, as if, from
now on, they will become the essence of my new life:

—Daddy's girl can crawl here.

The child repeats the game and, legs first, sinks back onto
the floor.

I pick her up again and put her back on the bed, grabbing her around the waist. She automatically goes on all fours,
crawls to the edge of the bed at full speed, then turns around
and sinks her legs down to the floor again. It takes her half a
minute to repeat the trick. By the fourth time I've picked her up
and put her down on the bed, she's getting tired and annoyed.
She's had enough of this game and is irritated by the limits I
keep placing on her freedom and exploration options. I'm tired,
too. Her mother hasn't been gone twenty minutes yet, and I've
already run out of ideas of things to do with the child. Don't

nine-month-old children ever potter about on their own for a
bit? I'm wondering if she should have a nap. Her mother said
she sleeps for three hours in the afternoon. Didn't I ask her how
often I needed to change her or did I forget? Did she answer me?
Isn't it time I changed her now?

Fifty-one

Half an hour later there's a knock on the door again. I think it might be my neighbor who has come to collect the iron I forgot to return to her yesterday. It's Anna again.

She wavers in the doorway with her case in her hands.

—I was just thinking, she says, casting her eyes to the floor, that's if you've no objections, of course, she continues as if trying to pave the way for what is about to follow, that I could just as easily finish the thesis here instead of going away. While you're getting to know each other, it's better for Flóra Sól as well, I mean, that she gets used to you while I'm here as well. That's if you've got nothing against it, she says, sounding insecure; she's feeling bad because she doesn't want to leave.

—Of course, I'd sleep on the sofa in the sitting room, she quickly adds, so you two could have the bedroom. Then she hesitantly steps in and bends over to pick up my daughter, who is playing with a cube, as if to emphasize that the child can't be without her. She takes a few steps back toward the door with the child, while she's waiting for my response and also because, formally speaking, I haven't invited her back in yet. Strictly speaking, she has already handed the child over to me. My daughter looks at her mother full of understanding, and I sense she's showing her solidarity; they're both staring at me from the door, the mother and daughter, waiting for my reaction.

—I could also stay in the guesthouse, she says, looking straight at the floor. She has a beautiful throat and neck.

—In any case I'd be at the library during the day.

Because I can see how bad she's feeling, the only thing that occurs to me is to put her mind at rest and gently touch her arm. Then I say:

—You can stay here, and there's a slight tremor in my voice.

I've just splattered it out without thinking about how quickly my life is changing.

—Thank you so much, she says softly. So long as you're sure it's OK. She's so clearly relieved, she almost looks happy.

First I offer her my bed and sleep on the sofa for one night, now I've just invited her to live with me and write her thesis. I should probably be asking myself what I just got myself into. What does it mean? That she is going to live with the child and me and teach me the ropes? And yet, deep inside, in some strange and indefinable way, I'm delighted.

—Would you like to just start on your thesis then while I take Flóra Sól out in the carriage? I say. You two can have the bedroom, I'll take the sofa, I add.

She grabs her case and takes it straight into the room. Then she reemerges with a thick book under her arm, sits down at the kitchen table, flicks through some chapters in the middle of the book, and starts reading her genetics.

Fifty-two

I suffered from earaches as a child, so I fasten the blue bonnet with the lace brim around my daughter before taking her out, ensuring, however, that her two curly locks remain visible. Then I set off with the child on a tour around the village. There is no denying that the baby carriage and I attract plenty of attention; the reception I get from the villagers is very different and a lot warmer when I'm with the child than when I'm on my own. I also notice something I'd never really thought about before, and that is that there are no children wandering around this place; I'm the only person with a small child in the village this morning.

I prop up my daughter so she can look back at the pedestrians who are watching her. She attracts both admiration and interest on our first trip down to the bottom of the main street. The women seem to give me more attention in my first fifteen minutes with the baby carriage than they have in the entire approximately two months I've been here alone in the village. Women's emotional lives seem pretty complex to me, and their reactions are often unpredictable. When I've finished pushing the carriage four times up and down the village street, I have the idea of taking my daughter into the church to show her the altarpiece with the baby Jesus that resembles her.

The uneven stonework on the floor causes the carriage to totter, so I leave it inside the church's entrance under a painting of doomsday and take the pacifier with me. Still, I don't expect anyone to object to the child being in the church, even if there is a mass going on. There are just a few old women on the benches. I don't walk straight to the picture with the child, but sit at the back to give my daughter a chance to acclimatize herself to the semidarkness. Then we gradually make our way toward the chancel at the front of the church and I show her the first paintings, one after another, reading out the inscriptions for her. We take our time with each painting; the child is interested and agile in my arms. We look at Mary Magdalene with her long red hair; then I halt when we get to Saint Joseph. The painting shows a careworn old man with drooping shoulders, weighed down by life's burdens. I put some coins in the box and light a candle. The inscription says that Saint Joseph was a loyal husband, as well as a devout and hardworking man. He was a foster father, I think to myself, and took on the responsibilities he was given. I'm not a foster father the way Joseph was; my daughter has the same kind of earlobes I have and a birthmark in the same spot of the groin. She's the flesh of my flesh, if I can put it in theological terms. Nevertheless I feel some sympathy for Saint Joseph; he must have felt lonely in bed.

—My brother Joseph, I say jokingly. Then I remember the postcard I was going to send to Jósef because he likes to collect stamps.

—It's a boy, I say when we reach Mary on the throne with her child. My daughter stops wriggling in my arms and becomes incredibly still and serious. She stares wide-eyed at her double with rosy cheeks, dimples, and two yellow curly locks on his forehead. Now that I'm standing here beside the painting with my daughter, I just can't get over the striking resemblance. Even the ears are the same; I hadn't noticed the folds in baby Jesus's ears before. A woman is kneeling in front of the painting and, when she stands up, glances back and forth at my daughter and the painting in wonderment. I know what's going through her mind.

On our way out I ask the woman who sells plastic saints in a little stall by the entrance for some more information about the painting. She says there are more questions than answers about it. Out of curiosity—and also because she's sometimes asked—she's tried to get some information on the piece, from Father Thomas among other people, but without any great results; there is even some uncertainty about who the painter is.

—It is generally believed, though, to be the work of a little-known woman painter, the daughter of a master from a neighboring province who has since been almost forgotten himself, says the woman handing my child a plastic saint to look at. The child pushes her small index finger through the gilded halo.

Fifty-three

My main concern right now is shopping for food. I didn't expect to have to cook more than one dinner for the mother and child and it's caught me off guard. Even though it hasn't exactly been said in so many words, I've been catapulted into family life with a woman and child sleeping in the next room. This isn't the result of any premeditated decision on my part, and I'm given no time to prepare myself. From now on I have to shop differently and cater to the needs of three people.

What might Anna like? Is she likely to prefer raspberry yogurt or forest berry yogurt? One should always be wary of a woman's interpretive skills. Still, Anna isn't likely to check the fat percentage and then to glare at me with disapproval, as you sometimes hear. If any conclusions can be drawn from last night's dinner it's that Anna eats anything that is put in front of her; she gobbled up the food and then had seconds.

—Is it OK if I finish it off? she asked when I'd finished eating, and she polished off the meat and sauce in the pan.

Although it isn't very practical to have to take the baby carriage everywhere, I have to admit that it's great to be able to load food on the rack and under the child's feet. I've no experience of buying food, but we start with fruit and I buy three of every kind because there are three of us in the home at the moment. I buy three apples, three oranges, three pears, three kiwis, and three bananas because Flóra Sól says *ba ba ba* and points at bananas. Then I add strawberries and raspberries. Next I buy another bag of potatoes because I have to think of dinner again. I'll probably end up cooking veal and boiling potatoes like yesterday. Even though I don't quite know how I'll cook them I also buy some different types of vegetables. The grocer pops everything I gradually point out to him into a paper bag and immediately scribbles some figures on a sheet. I follow the same method for the vegetables, three tomatoes, three onions, three peppers, and three pieces of some violet thing that might be a vegetable or a fruit, I'm not sure.

As I'm coming out of the butcher's with the veal, I meet Father Thomas. He greets me with a handshake, and then he just can't take his eyes off the child, as if he is discovering a new reality. Flóra Sól gets all excited and lets me know that she wants to get out of the carriage and meet the priest. I pick her up and hold her in my arms as we chat, as if to assert my role as a father. My daughter smiles at Father Thomas, and he pats her on the head; then she goes all shy and lays her head on my shoulder.

—A beautiful and intelligent child, he says. The pair of you together have probably lowered the average age demographic in this village; there aren't many young people around here.

I tell the priest that I won't be coming to the garden for another two to three days, but that I'll be back, I'll be getting a babysitter for a few hours in the afternoon. I don't mention Anna because that would complicate things, and I haven't told her about the garden yet.

—Brother Matthew is going to water the plants while you're away, says the priest.

Before I know it I've asked him if he knows any food recipes.

—Nothing too complicated, I say, I don't have much experience. Then I tell him that I did veal in red wine sauce yesterday and that it went down well, and that I have veal again tonight. After that I need to start varying it a bit.

My question doesn't seem to throw the priest in the least, or he doesn't show it if it does. He says he never actually cooks himself, but he can think of a few films that might be good for me to watch. If he were to mention the first ones that come to mind they would be *The Cook, the Thief, His Wife & Her Lover*, which is actually fairly unconventional and doesn't really apply in this case; *Eat Drink Man Woman*; *Chocolat*; *Babette's Feast*; *Like Water for Chocolate*; *Chungking Express*; and *In the Mood for Love*, he says, apologizing for his translations of the titles, because he's quoting them loosely from memory.

One of the movies focuses especially on a chocolate confectionary. The basic theme is the struggle between good and evil, with the parish priest as the baddie and the woman who makes the chocolates representing the forces of good, says Father Thomas chirpily, as he fleetingly greets an old woman walking by.

—They don't really go into measurements and proportions, he adds, but these films can still put me on the right track when it comes to cooking. He says that my daughter and I are welcome to pop by when we've finished shopping and check out his videos.

Since the shopping is formally done and my daughter and I don't strictly speaking have anything special to do, we follow him back to the guesthouse. He takes some films off the shelf and lines them up on the desk; then choosing one movie, he opens the case and slips the tape into the VCR. Father Thomas says no director depicts the love of food like this one, but it takes him several minutes to find the scene he thinks might guide me in my cooking. Meanwhile my daughter watches him with interest.

Asian faces appear on the screen, women with great hairdos and beautiful dresses. The scene Father Thomas chooses for me is about two minutes long and shows people carrying noodle soup in buckets down narrow corridors and damp passageways.

The next film the priest chooses is an opening scene in which the hero is slaughtering a hen with a sharp knife and preparing a very elaborate meal in an incredibly short time. The thing that draws my attention in this film is the hero's beautiful collection of knives; hundreds of razor-sharp implements cover the entire wall of the kitchen in the background. The priest takes the tape out and slips a third video into the machine. He fast-forwards a moment, then rewinds, and looks hesitantly over his shoulder at my nine-month-old daughter:

—This one isn't suitable for children, he says.

Fifty-four

On the way home it occurs to me to look into a small children's clothes shop next to the barber's. I spot a floral dress in the window that might fit my daughter. The furnishings are archaic and the children's clothes a bit old-fashioned. The owner of the shop is an old woman, close to ninety. She's happy to get some customers into the shop and immediately pulls out two floral dresses, one with blue checkerberries, the other with pink roses. I stand Flóra Sól up on the counter and loosely measure up the dresses against her. Still, I'm not sure the designs suit a person whose body is mainly built around the waist. Then the woman remembers a yellow dress she has stored away in a special place at the back, with a pattern of white lilies, an irresistible crocheted lace collar, and crocheted yellow stockings to match. I go for it and buy the floral dress and stockings. As I'm about to pay, the woman points out that my daughter needs a coat to go with the dress and says she'll give me a good discount. She returns quickly with one wrapped in plastic, tiny, a burgundy woolen coat with double lining and a stitched collar and pockets. I put the coat on my daughter and stand her back up on the counter. She is undeniably short in this full-length coat, but the color suits her as she stands there upright on the counter, looking like a porcelain doll in a museum, a miniature adult. Some more people have come into the shop, and my daughter wins the admiration of two of the shop owner's elderly lady friends who have popped in. I walk out with the burgundy coat, yellow dress, and stockings.

In the evening I cook veal in wine sauce again, but instead of frying the meat in slices, I chop it into pieces and make a veal goulash for the mother of my child and nine-month-old daughter. Then I boil the potatoes like the night before, only this time I mash them.

After dinner I put my daughter into the dress and coat to show them to her mother. The child repeats the performance she gave in the shop on the kitchen table and claps her hands in approval.

Anna laughs and claps back, admiring her daughter for a moment, and then sinks back into her book. I'm a bit worried about how absentminded she can be when she's with the child; she plays with her daughter for brief spells, they frolic about, laugh and titter, but then it's as if her mind is totally elsewhere and she loses interest, hands me the child, sits at the kitchen table, and opens her books. Although I don't think she's more interested in her research than Flóra Sól, I do nevertheless worry about how fleeting her cheerful moments can be.

Fifty-five

There's no such thing as a normal day, and everything, literally everything, that is connected to my role as a father is new to me. In the evening, for the first time, I experiment with giving the child a bath. Since hot water is in short supply and the water pressure is so low that it takes an eternity to run a bath, I try placing my daughter in a reasonably large sink and bathe her there.

She's into running water in a big way and is having fun in the sink with a small plastic cup, which she fills and immediately empties. Before long I'm drenched and the floor is flooded. The easiest thing to do would be to take the child with me when I'm having a bath myself, and make better use of the water that way. The only snag, though, is that once I've shampooed her hair and rinsed her two golden curls, someone has to take the child out of my bathwater. When I've finished bathing her in the sink, I wrap a towel around her small, soft body and then comb her hair with a soft brush. I realize I could place a ribbon in her hair to match the yellow dress. I look up the word in the dictionary and write it down.

—Tomorrow we'll buy a ribbon and put it in your hair, I say to my daughter.

—Do, do, she says loud and clear.

I put her in her pajamas, fastening its only two buttons, one over her belly button and the other below her throat. Then I display the smiling, wet-combed child to my friend, who is still stooped over a book at the kitchen table. I give her mom a chance to admire the fruit of her creation, the fruit of our creation.

She acknowledges the child, gives her a brief smile, and plants a kiss on one of her dimples.

—Is she in new pajamas? she asks.

—Yeah, we bought them together today, when we went into the village, I say, lifting my daughter onto the table so that her mom can see the pink two-piece flannel pajamas with green rabbits.

—Nice, she says, nodding at me to add weight to her words, very nice; but instead of looking at her child she looks at me with her aquamarine eyes. Flóra Sól stretches out her arms toward her mother for a hug; then she immediately rests her head on my shoulder, she wants to go to bed.

—Sleep, the model child repeats in her clear voice.

I tuck my child into the cot that the monks brought me. I'm still puzzled by how Father Thomas managed to track down the bed. Even though I've drawn the curtains closed, it's as if there's always a strange light around the child. Several people have commented on the light around my daughter, even on a cloudy day like today, including the lady on the top floor when I returned the iron to her.

It doesn't take long to put Flóra Sól to sleep, and by the time I'm finished, Anna is completely immersed in her scientific studies at the kitchen table. I see that she's washed up and picked up the child's toys. I think of asking her if she wants to go out for the evening and have a look around. I could draw a map of the village for her with the main street and our street running through it; that would be two lines, the sign of a cross in fact, then I could mark two or three places that she could perhaps have a closer look at, the church, town hall, post office, and the café beside it, it wouldn't take long. Will it seem like I am trying to get rid of her, that I'm afraid of being left alone with her when Flóra Sól is asleep? What if she gets lost or someone accosts her? Instead I sit facing her at the table, and all of a sudden I feel the need to tell her something personal about my life that she doesn't know yet.

I fetch a photograph of Jósef and myself and show her. We're standing side by side in the garden, but unusually I'm not holding his hand.

—This isn't a relative? she asks.

The question doesn't surprise me, Jósef is a head smaller than I am and looks totally unlike me. It's a natural first reaction. It isn't his looks, though, that make Jósef unlike other people. At first sight, he looks like a very handsome young man with his dark hair, brown eyes, and tanned skin, like he's just stepped off a beach. Lots of women are charmed by him, even after they realize that he doesn't talk. Because I was so often reminded of how handsome my brother was, I assumed that I was somehow the opposite.

—We're actually twins.

She looks me straight in the eye. Her eyes are very unusual, more turquoise than aquamarine.

—What do you mean by actually twins?

—Yeah, we weren't in fact born on the same day, but we're still twins, we were together in the womb. It's true, I was born first, my brother two hours later, just after midnight the next day. So technically speaking we're twins and celebrate our birthdays on the same day, my birthday, the ninth of November.

—You've never mentioned a brother. I thought you were an only child.

—Yeah, but I do have a brother. He moved into a community home when Mom died. They don't know what's wrong with him; there have been conflicting diagnoses, probably some kind of faulty connection in the brain and autism. He doesn't talk, he's the quiet one in the family. People who don't know about it often don't notice anything; they're so happy to have found a good listener, I say with a smile.

Anna nods; she seems to have an understanding and a genuine interest in what I have to say about Jósef. She asks for more details about the diagnosis, and I sense that we're entering her home ground now, the field of genetics. She closes the thick book and doesn't leave her pencil in it. I get the feeling that's not just temporary, that she's stopped studying for the night.

—He behaves quite normally somehow and can cope quite well. He greets people with a handshake and is always well turned out and tidy, although he sometimes wears some pretty wild colors.

In the photograph I'm showing to Anna he's in a violet shirt with butterfly patterns—the last shirt Mom bought for him—and a mint-green tie.

—Dad and I put the ties on him; he can't do the knots himself. When he stays over on weekends he always carefully folds his clothes and puts them in his old wardrobe, even when he's only staying for one night. Three minutes after he's up his bed is made, all smooth and without a crease, like a hotel room that's been tidied by three maids.

Anna wants to know more about the system my twin brother has developed for himself.

—His whole life is based on fixed routines, I say. When my brother visits on weekdays, he always wants to do the same things, to make popcorn, and then he wants to dance with me.

On the first weekend he stayed with us after Mom died, he seemed a bit standoffish and insecure. He was used to Mom taking care of him and fussing around him, and he went out to the greenhouse to look for her several times. By the next time, though, he knew the system had changed and seemed to adapt to the new circumstances. He'd created a new system.

—He actually has a great capacity to adapt, I say.

Anna nods; she knows what I'm getting at. I grab the bottle of wine and pour two glasses.

—The main thing that distinguishes my twin brother from other people is that he never changes mood; in fact he's practically always happy, I say, it's genuine happiness, like a colored light bulb over a hall door, and he's fascinated by the beauty of the world. He's a very good person, I say finally, he's incapable of lying.

I smile. She smiles, too.

—What about you? Do you lie sometimes? she asks, looking straight at me.

She throws me off guard; I can feel my heart beating under my sweater.

—No, but maybe I don't always say what I'm thinking, I answer.

Later that night I make the sofa bed again. Once I'm under the covers, I try not to be bothered by the fact that my female friend is sleeping in a bed that's far too big for her, at a mere arm's length from me. Instead I try to focus on tomorrow's meals. I'm wondering if I could pull off a dessert and whether Mom's recipe for cocoa soup might be a good idea.

Fifty-six

It's been three days since the girls fell unexpectedly into my life, so to speak, and this is the first time we're going out together with the child in the carriage. We have a specific mission: I'm going to show the mother of my child where the library is. Anna has changed the carriage into a stroller and we alternate pushing it. Our daughter is in her flowery yellow dress and has a ribbon in her hair. People are staring at us so I feel like announcing to everyone that we're not a couple and that just because we're taking our child for a stroll doesn't mean that we sleep together, that this is just a temporary setup.

The library is beside the café, but before Anna dives back into her science, we sit down at one of the three tables on the sidewalk, facing each other with the stroller between us. I put on the brake while Anna adjusts our daughter, ties the laces that have come loose around her hat, and hands the child a strawberry, which she immediately shoves into her mouth. An older couple is sitting at the next table, and I hear the man say he'll have the same thing his wife is having. Is that the sign of a successful relationship? Ordering the same thing? Should I also say I'll have the same thing that Anna, the mother of my child, is having? I practice several potential answers in the local dialect in my mind; the onus is on me to speak for both of us, since I'm the one who's been living in the village for two months.

—One coffee, says Anna, smiling at the owner.

—Same for me, I say.

My daughter claps her hands in excitement and parrots my last syllable.

If the owner of the café asks me straight out if she's my girl-friend, I'll deny it.

—Is that your girlfriend?

But he doesn't.

Before the owner goes in for the coffees, he stoops over the child, doting over her, and then gently pinches her cheek and pats her on the head. People seem to be very child-friendly here; practically no one leaves the child alone. And the men have been eyeing up Anna, too, I can't help noticing. I also realize that the child attracts less attention when her mother is with her. I have mixed feelings about this, even though, just a few minutes ago, I was worried that people might think we were a couple.

The man who is squatting on the steps of the library is star-ing at Anna so intensively that it's almost rude, I feel like telling him to stop it. Instead I lift my daughter out of the stroller and sit her on my knee by the table. She's all fidgety, but doesn't touch the coffee cups. I stick the pacifier in her but she spits it right out. She tries to stand on my knees, and I lift her up so that she can see all around her. She waves at the man on the steps and he waves back. Then I try putting her on the empty chair beside me, let her sit on her own chair between us parents, with her head just about reaching over the edge of the table. We both look at her proudly, the parents; inside my head I'm turning into the father of a little child. Her mother smiles at me. I hope the guy on the library steps also noticed the smile. This is how my new life comes into being, this is how the reality of it is created.

Fifty-seven

It's nine a.m., Anna has just gone to the library, and my daughter and I have been up for an hour and a half. I haven't mentioned the garden to Anna, but I will soon need to go back up there to water the plants. I don't trust Brother Matthew with these things anymore; he's in his nineties.

Taking care of a child is a lot of work; you can never keep any particular train of thought going for long. When the child's awake I need to give her my full attention. I'm probably a little bit clumsy with my daughter, and I can't do things the way her mother can, but she takes it all in her stride. But I try to manage my role as a father as best I can, by doing what's necessary and being consistent with myself. Then I try to be good to the child while I wait for Anna to come back from the library.

Although the child is almost always happy, that doesn't mean she can't be temperamental. But her temperament isn't determined by my moods or any other factors in her surroundings. Was I a cheerful child, I wonder? Dad spent more time with Jósef than with me, and Mom and I were more of a pair, too.

Then there's another side to my daughter when she wants to be left to her own devices, in peace and without being disturbed. She can acquire a serious air in those moments and even frown. She sometimes even crawls into the bedroom and tries to close the door behind her, or she finds a spot where she thinks no one will see her. I keep one eye on her from a distance but otherwise leave her be.

—My little hermit, I say when she crawls back out of her cell ready to embrace the world again.

There are many fun and interesting things about this little being. The way she whistles, for example. I noticed this morning that she was trying to purse her lips, checking them in the mirror several times from where she was sitting on the floor in the bedroom. Once that target has been achieved, my nine-month-old daughter pumps her lungs with air and blows through the spout. As soon as she produces a pure tone, she becomes startled, but when I smile at her, she wants to show me more and forms a new spout and blows again.

—Clever girl. Incredibly clever girl.

—Should Daddy sing and Flóra Sól whistle with him?

She's ecstatic, I'm an ecstatic father, and I'm dying to share my fatherly pride with Anna when she gets back from the library. I also wish Mom could see her granddaughter; I wish she could see me in my role as a father. How would Mom haven taken to Anna?

I pick the child up off the floor and put her in her floral dress with her blue cardigan over it. Then I put a sun hat on her and let her look at herself in the mirror again before I put her into the carriage. She thinks it's fun to dress up.

—Shall we go out in the carriage and see Daddy's roses? Would Flóra Sól like to go to the garden with Daddy and meet the monks and look at the *Rosa candida*?

I plug the pacifier into her when we get out with the carriage, spread a blanket over her, and she quickly falls asleep.

When I get to the steps leading up to the rose garden, I take her out of the carriage, with the blanket and pillow and climb the hill with the child in my arms. Once we reach the garden, I put her down on the blanket on the grass right beside me while I work in the flower beds. My daughter sleeps another hour. I move her twice with me around the garden as I switch patches and always keep her within reach.

Then she's suddenly awake and is sitting up, visibly puzzled by her surroundings. She looks all around her, sees me, and breaks into a big smile. Then she sets off, abandoning the blanket for the divine green nature.

—Don't you want me to change Daddy's girl's diaper? I ask, taking off my gardening gloves. Once I've changed her, I sit with her on the garden bench and give her pear juice to drink from a spout cup.

—Do you want to smell the scent?

The shorter, full-blown roses are the same height as her, and she shows a lot of interest in the flowers. Right beside her there is a red-pink rosebud, which she first gently skims with her index before bending her neck to sniff the flower with a theatrical gesture and to finally gasp in wonderment. I burst out laughing. Then I realize that Brother Jacob and Brother Matthew have made their way out of the library into the garden. I don't know how long they've been standing there for, watching us, but they both have beaming smiles. They then rally up more brothers, and by the end, there are eleven of them; the only one missing is Brother Zacharias. They want Flóra Sól to give a repeat performance of sniffing the rose. The child enjoys being in the limelight and continues her act without further ado. The monks laugh for a good while. I'm a little bit stressed about having the child in the garden; it's considered to be within the walls of the monastery, and I never intended to stop there for long.

Brother Michael vanishes and swiftly returns with a ball in his hands; it's the size of a football, except that it's pink and has the picture of a dolphin on it, as far as I can make out. They confer on how best to organize the game so that the child can be in the middle and come to the conclusion that it's best to place it on the lawn and very slowly roll the ball toward the child. My daughter titters and laughs and claps her hands. She's quick to grasp the rules of the game. I see her stroking Brother Paul's bald head. Before going home I clip a bunch of roses to take with me. It occurs to me as I'm giving the child a piggyback down the steps that I must remember to ask Brother Gabriel for his vegetable soup recipe.

As soon as the bouquet of roses is in water in the middle of the kitchen table, I feel it was a bit rash of me to come home with all those roses. I must at least make it clear that the roses are from the child to the mother.

I discuss the garden with Anna in the evening, once I've put the child to bed. I tell her I'm trying to save a centuries-old rose garden, with some unique species, from neglect and abandonment.

—Your dad didn't mention any work in the garden, she says.

—Many species are in danger of extinction, I say, and that'll reduce the flora, I add, a point of view the genetics expert should well understand.

—Yeah, she says, it's no problem to split the day so that I'll be with Flóra Sól in the afternoons while you go to the garden. Instead I'll do a bit of studying in the evenings, when she's asleep, if that's OK by you.

Fifty-eight

There is a temporary understanding between us with regard to the housekeeping and upbringing of our daughter. After offering to cook the meal on the first day, I never had to mention it again; by the second day, it was already an established pattern in our cohabitation that I would do the cooking. The division of tasks in my new family life has been set right from the word *go*; I assume the genetics expert knew even less about cooking than I did. Still though, she does her share of shopping and often comes home from the library with all kinds of cakes and tarts from the bakery. Because I haven't managed to learn any more recipes in such a short time, I'm cooking veal in wine sauce for the third evening in a row. This time I carve the meat into streaks, to make a change from the goulash we had the night before, and fry it in spring onions. Then I try to boil various types of vegetables with the potatoes: carrots, peas, and spinach, and they don't taste bad with the sauce. The mother and daughter never complain; the child eats the carrot-spinach mash and well-chopped meat with great appetite, and Anna gobbles up the dinner for the third evening in a row and helps herself to seconds. And yet she's skinny; she's so lean you can see her ribs through her T-shirt and her hips through her jeans. I'm determined to fatten her up while she's under my roof and to turn her into a rotund mother. The first thing I have to do is learn more recipes, of course, and the next day I ask everyone I meet on my path about food. The butcher advises me to try more types of meat, but I decide not to chance it just yet, so he teaches me how to make cream sauce instead of red wine sauce.

—If you put cream on the pan instead of red wine, you'll get a thick, light brown sauce; if you continue to use wine the sauce will be thin and red-brown. You decide.

I also go into the bookshop and skim through two cookbooks. They're written in the village dialect and, as far as I can make out, one of them is only about squid recipes. The books look old; you can see it from the clothes the people standing by the banquet tables are wearing, and the colors of the food look gaudy and odd.

In the end I go to the woman in the restaurant and ask her to teach me one or two dishes. I take the child with me everywhere I go to reduce the likelihood of being sent on a fool's errand. The woman searches for some garlic and tells me that once you know how to use garlic, you know how to cook food. She pulls a whole string of garlic off the wall, chooses some cloves, and makes me practice opening them.

—First you peel them, then slice them into pieces and crush them.

She makes me repeat all this several times and tells me that I'm obviously a good learner. While I'm handling the garlic on the carving board, she offers to hold the child. Then she wants to teach me how to cook squid: Slice it into pieces, heat some oil, and chuck it into the pot, she says twice, forcing me to repeat it after her. She asks me what I can cook and I tell her about the veal and potatoes and sauce.

—Instead of the potatoes you can boil some rice, she says, one cup of rice for every cup of water, turn the heat off when the water boils, and let it simmer under the lid for ten minutes. She repeats that twice as well. When I'm about to thank her for the help, she disappears into the kitchen a moment and comes straight back with a bowl, which she hands to me.

—Plum pie, she says. You can have it for dessert. I could also cook for you if need be and you could take it home.

Then she asks me if she can hold the child again for a short while, and I allow her to. Flóra Sól pats the woman's cheeks with her short chubby fingers; then she places her palm flat over the woman's head for a very brief moment, like a priest blessing a child.

On our way home I pop into the butcher's to buy some more veal. Once he's carved the slices for me, I point at the mincing machine behind him. This time I ask him to mince the meat because I'm going to make some meatballs. I've already decided I'm going to clip some herbs on the balcony and make a cream sauce with them to go with the meat.

As we're walking by the phone booth, I remember that I haven't spoken to Dad for two weeks. I lift Flóra Sól out of the carriage and hold her as I call him. I don't expect Dad to ask me about my plans for the future while the girls are with me. Here I am, cast in the role of a child's father and the father of a woman's child; that's about as close as I can get to defining my current role in life.

—Shall we ring Granddad?

—Gram-da.

Dad is happy to hear from me and immediately asks about the girls, especially how Anna's thesis is going. I can hear that he's well informed about her field of research, either through conversations he's had with my child's mother, whom he's been meeting without my knowledge, or else he's been reading up on the subject.

—I pointed out an interesting article to her on the ethics of genetic research, says the electrician.

Since I have him on the line, I ask Dad about the meatballs Mom used to make. He doesn't remember the recipe, but thinks she mixed egg and rusk with the minced meat. Then he says that he was invited over to Bogga's for coffee yesterday.

—She had quite a selection of biscuits, good old Bogga: half-moon cookies, Jewish cakes, and what-have-you.

Talking to Dad triggers off all kinds of emotions. There's always a chance of some hidden meaning behind the things he says, that what he really wants to say is lurking several layers below the surface.

When I come home carrying the shopping and my daughter in my arms, my elderly neighbor from the top floor is out on the landing.

I think it's no coincidence that every time I'm either on my way in or out with the child, my neighbor suddenly finds something to do outside her apartment. When the child isn't with me she goes straight back in again. At first, I thought she might be trying to make some kind of statement on the owner's behalf: that there were now three of us and not two in the apartment. But she seems relieved to see us, as if she'd been waiting for us. What she wants is to say hello to my daughter, she's learned her name now, Fló-ra Sól, she says, coming down three steps to meet us. Then the woman pats the child and strokes her, and the child pats her back. Finally, the woman wants to know if I need the iron again. Or the whisk? My daughter smiles at her.

—Since this child has moved into the building my eczema is much better; it's practically vanished from my hands and it's diminished on my legs, says the woman on the landing, pulling up the fold of her dress slightly.

✳

Fifty-nine

I try to be up and have the sofa bed folded back before the girls come in. We've divided our time so that I'm with the child until two o'clock, while Anna is at the library; then the girls are together in the afternoon while I go to the garden. So basically we've split the day into three shifts: mornings, afternoons, and evenings.

Flóra Sól is sitting in the cot looking at a picture book and does not therefore require my undivided attention. This gives me a bit of time to think things over, to have a better look at the plan I found in the library during the week, to organize and draw up a list of tasks for the next few days. If the original drawing is anything to go by, the garden was created with symmetrical patterns that subtly blended in with the soft lines of nature; the essence of the botanical art was the interplay between light and shadow. Then it seems that the rose beds were organized in octagonal plots around the pond and a lot of potherbs and healing herbs were planted in a special herb garden. The drawing also shows various types of jars and tubs that were used to store the healing herbs and spices.

I nevertheless glance at Flóra Sól every now and then, and she sometimes looks up from her book at me. It's a volume of biblical parables for children with a picture on each page and very few words. She manages to browse through the book by herself, carefully peeling back each page with her thumb and index, and always stops on the same picture of a king brandishing a sword and holding up a child that two women are claiming as their own. I wonder if the book is too violent for the child. I was touched by the gift, though, and surprised when I saw Brother Matthew appear with a book under his arm while I was planting.

Innumerable quarters of an hour go by in this manner. I change my daughter, dress her, talk to her, build a tower out of letter cubes with her or assemble a thirteen-piece jigsaw, sing with her, feed her, wash her face, put her into her outdoor clothes, and off we go to buy some food and take a stroll. Or we go to the café and keep our eyes open in case we meet Anna. Then we go into the church every day to look at the picture of baby Jesus. We always follow the same routine and don't walk straight up to the painting, but rather approach it slowly. First we take one round and look at the other paintings and light a candle for Joseph. My daughter bounces with excitement and joy in my arms; she knows what's coming. I get the feeling she's put on weight since she and her mother moved in, she's starting to sink in my arms. Has Anna put on some weight, too, I wonder?

The same thing always happens when we get to the painting of Mary on her throne with the baby Jesus; the child stops bouncing in my arms, becomes serious and perfectly still, and looks at the child in the picture with big eyes.

I'm not a strict father and am incapable of scolding a child, although I realize I have to growl every now and then to prevent Flóra Sól from doing herself any harm. Still, I feel my daughter is totally guileless and shows the world an unnecessary amount of affection; she wants to pat and caress every single creature she meets on her path. I have to admit her fearlessness and boundless kindness are a source of concern to me.

—No, no, I say in a deep, responsible voice when a skinny, raggedy alley cat approaches outside the church.

—Aaaaaaaaah, says the child tenderly, stretching out her arms toward the animal and signaling me to release her from my arms so that she can be on the same level as the wild animal. She wants to hug the cat the same way she hugs strangers. The child shows all living and moving creatures nothing but warmth and trust. Considering how precocious my daughter is in other areas—she already has a considerable vocabulary in her mother tongue and a few words in Latin, in addition to several words she's picked up in the local dialect, like how to say hello and bye—I'm a little bit irritated by the fact that my nine-month-old daughter isn't a better judge of character when it comes to being friendly with strangers and wanting to be good to scraggy alley cats.

The cat has big green eyes and rubs up against my leg.

—No, no, not allowed to touch.

And next you say:

—Didn't I warn you, my little darling, that wild cats scratch, didn't I? Didn't I warn you four times before I was forced to put you in the carriage again?

A father's worries about his guileless daughter are not unnatural when there are wild animals involved. I pick up the child and say:

—No, no, ugly cat, in a grave voice.

My daughter has stopped smiling; she looks at me with her big, deep, calm eyes and pale porcelain face. She seems fearless but baffled. I feel an immediate rush of guilt.

The animal looks at me with her sensitive feline eyes.

—OK, be good to the pussycat, I say with mixed feelings and little conviction, as I kneel down beside the scruffy cat with my child. Let's give pussy something to eat, I say, reaching into the shopping bag for some appropriate cat food.

—Come on, I then say to my daughter, I'll show you the distinction between good and bad.

I go back into the church and place her on a high chair in the semidarkness so that she can see the pictures high up. I can't see her expression, but I know she is focused on the sculptures with serious and concentrated eyes, that she understands that at the top of every pillar there is a representation of the final conflict between good and evil, the fight between angels and demons, guilt and innocence, it's all there clearly carved in stone: horns and hooves, halos, cowering faces, and benign expressions.

—Do you understand now, child, the evils of the world and man?

At first she clenches fistfuls of hair in both of her baby hands, then she slides her small palms over my forehead and holds them over my eyes a moment. She has a grip on my ears now, and finally I feel her patting my cheeks, first one and then she caresses the other.

When we get home and I'm folding the carriage, and my daughter is sitting at the bottom of the stairs, I notice that there are two women waiting for us on the landing, our elderly neighbor with a visiting friend, a woman of the same age. Her friend has asthma and wants to meet my daughter because she's heard my neighbor talk so much about her. She's told her the story of the vanishing eczema and now the friend wants to see the child. I'm given no peace. I'd rather Anna didn't find out about the interest strangers are showing in her daughter and that people are slipping me jars of jam and dried spicy sausage every time I take her out.

—Were you buying cat food? my child's mother asks me when I come home and she pulls three cans out of the shopping bag.

Sixty

I'm trying to figure out what makes a woman tick and come to the conclusion that Anna's emotional life is considerably more complex and varied than that of the guys I know. She sometimes looks worried, but the thing that puzzles me the most is how distant she can seem, as if she isn't actually here, as if she is tackling several problems at once. Even though she might only be sitting forty centimeters away from me, on the other side of the table, so close in fact that if we were a couple I would be able to kiss her without having to move, it's as if she doesn't notice me.

Apart from that she's considerate and warm and often smiles at me and praises me every evening for my cooking, and it's not as if she doesn't put her books down when I'm talking to her. She seems happy to see us when my daughter and I come through the door, but then after a short while she sinks back into her books again.

She does sometimes look at me when I'm playing with the child, although I'm not sure whether she's looking at me as much as I'm looking at her. She's probably examining me with my daughter from a genetic point of view. I have my suspicion confirmed when I turn the loaf of bread around on the carving board.

—Are you left-handed? she asks, looking at me with interested aquamarine eyes.

Because we're temporarily living under the same roof and it's a small apartment, we sometimes have to squeeze past each other, so we occasionally accidentally touch. I've also deliberately stroked her once and twice. I think of the body just as much as before, but try to limit it to those hours when Anna is not around, like when I'm working in the garden. I'm so afraid that my thoughts will become externally visible. Anna might be one of those women who can see images of people's thoughts before they've even thought them themselves, hovering over their heads in frilly steam bubbles. Mom was like that, could read my thoughts. I certainly want to have Anna as a friend, but the fact that she's a woman and we have a child together undeniably complicates things. When we're in the same room, the mother of my child and I, I feel I'm constantly losing the thread of our conversations. Especially if she's just out of the shower with wet hair or has slipped a hairpin in it to keep it off her face. It isn't until I'm under the covers, alone with my soul, and the girls are asleep in the next room that I feel I can allow myself to think of the body; it reminds me yet once more that I'm alive. I'll admit that I have entertained the possibility that something might spark off between Anna and me, something other than a new life, I mean. The thing that saves me from the narrow alley of physical yearnings is the open kitchen window. From the pillow, my direct line of vision through the darkness outside leads to the insurmountable monastery wall, behind which, on the side of the slumbering vineyard, are my rose beds, which I must water tomorrow. I'm the only man who knows about a certain type of resilient rose out there in the darkness under the yellow moon.

Sixty-one

The child is developing incredibly fast. Every moment spent together, every morning while the mother of my child is immersed in some new genetic pool at the library, is a time when great strides are made and stupendous victories are won. When Anna comes home the achievements of the day are replayed. It's something to look forward to all morning, that's what the game is all about, being able to experience her wonderment and enchantment and receive confirmation that something important has taken place here while she was at the library, that I've been witness to a wonderful miracle which will now be repeated.

The heir to my greenhouse is standing on the floor in her stockings and holding onto the double bed with both hands. I'm looking for her sweater on the other side of the room when I notice a concentrated expression on her face as she first unclenches her minute fingers and lets go of one hand and then the other, carefully and yet, at the same time, strangely secure. Then she stands still for several moments, unsupported on the floor in front of the bed, her tummy out, before she sets off, boldly and confidently into the unknown, for a total of three steps. She holds her arms in the air to keep her balance; there are dimples on her knees.

When Anna gets home, I grab our daughter from the floor where she is sitting piling up letter cubes, tearing her away from a half-finished Tower of Babel, and stand her in the middle of the floor, like a strolling player in the middle of a square premiering a divine comedy. First I hold both her hands and then gradually release my grip, one finger at a time. Initially she stands there in the middle of the kitchen floor with an incredibly concentrated air, and then the miracle occurs; she shifts all her body weight onto one leg so that she can lift the other one off the floor and quickly turns it into a step forward. Then she repeats the process with the other leg and takes a total of four steps forward with growing confidence, by swinging her hips like a little robot. Her mother kneels to catch her and lifts her up in a tight embrace and cuddles her. I watch her hugging the child; that's made my day, at least. I calmly wait for the mother of my offspring to express her amazement at the day's achievements. I don't have to wait long for a reaction.

—That's incredible, she's started to walk. You've taught her so many things, to sing loads of songs, to whistle, to put a twenty-piece jigsaw puzzle together, and now to walk.

She's still tightly hugging the child. Although I'm touched by Anna's joy, it's like she's in some kind of slight emotional over-drive. She seems agitated.

—I just feel it's so much at once, to give birth to a child and then the next day she's walking, and then the next thing you know she's left home and maybe phones you once in a blue moon, and you've got no more say in the matter. There are tears in her eyes.

—Now, now, I say. It's a bit far-fetched to say that she's leav-ing home. It's not as if I'm about to escort our daughter down the aisle.

—Sorry, says Anna, Flóra Sól is a wonderful child and I feel it's so much responsibility being a mother. She hands me the child and dabs her tears.

—I wasn't this worried before I had Flóra Sól. Now I'm wor-ried about everything, I'm even afraid that you might not come back when you got out to the shop to buy goulash veal or to meet your film buff.

I've no control over my thoughts, because all of a sudden I long to sleep with her. I'm so troubled by my impulses that I immediately dress the child in her anorak and hood. I was supposed to be going to the garden, but instead I suddenly rush out with the child, without explanation. I feel the urge to be outside to grab a hold of myself. Still though, since we were, after all, intimate for a quarter of a night just a year and a half ago, it shouldn't be such an incredibly big step to take.

Sixty-two

Then sometimes we all sit at the table together, Anna, the child, and I, and all are focused on our own things. I fuse my role as a father with my other interest and grab a large gardening book with two thousand five hundred species of plants in it and sit down with my daughter opposite Anna, and we browse through the book together.

I quickly skim over the chapters about plant diseases and pests, and also over the chapters on lawns and bushes, before stopping on the chapter about the building of ponds and streams in gardens, which my daughter seems to be particularly interested in. We focus mainly on the illustrations and skip the text pages. The child places three of her chubby little fingers on one of the pictures. I wonder what the monks will say about the pond, which is almost ready. Sitting opposite us, less than an arm's length away, the child's mother is totally immersed in how genetic characteristics are passed on between generations and doesn't seem to be aware of our proximity. We move from streams to drawing room plants.

—Some of the most beautiful plants in the world grow around here, I say to my daughter. But back in our country you can only grow them in the sitting room window facing south. Around here, under the open sky, I repeat the words, trying to express the same ideas in different ways. That's my contribution to the development of my nine-month-old daughter's linguistic skills, to make her understand that reality can be approached in different ways.

—By the most beautiful plants in the world, I mostly mean roses, I say to the child.

Anna looks up from the book and observes me for a short moment as if she were trying to solve a riddle. Flóra Sól and I take notes. I mark the most important information with a cross and then put down my pencil. My daughter stretches out for the pencil and also draws a clear cross on the same page. My child's mother looks up from her research; something has attracted her attention.

—There's no question about it, she's left-handed like you, she says.

The geneticist points at the child, who is holding the pencil in her left hand like her father. Her interest in her daughter and me seems to have suddenly increased. Since it so happens that I have the book open to a page about the hybridization of roses and cross-fertilization in nature, I wonder if I should mention plant genetics or plant biotechnology; it could be a way of fusing our fields of interest, the DNA of plants. Instead I ask what she's engrossed in.

—What about you, what are you reading? I ask, and my daughter also looks up. We both look over the table at Anna with interest. She gives a brief summary of the research material, as if she only had a limited interest in the subject. In fact, you could say that she summarizes the whole thing in just one phrase:

—Deoxyribonucleic acid, she says and smiles at us.

—De-o, says the child quite clearly, standing up in my arms.

—Yeah, we'll go to the church later, I say to my daughter.

—Why do you say that? Anna asks, giving us both a bewildered look in turn.

—It's Latin for god I explain. Our daughter doesn't only speak her mother tongue, I add in a lighter tone, she's a nine-and-a-half-month-old girl and she already speaks two languages.

We both laugh. I'm relieved.

—Are you teaching the child Latin?

I tell Anna that we go to the church to look at an old painting of a baby Jesus that looks like our daughter.

—Apart from that there actually isn't an awful lot that we can do around here.

My daughter is tuned in and wants to show her mother more things she's learned in the church, and lifts up three fingers like the child in the painting. She's wearing a light blue elbow-sleeve blouse, with dimples on her elbows. Then she draws a clear cross in the air. I give Anna a sideways glance; I don't know how she's taking this pantomime. We've occasionally stumbled into some of Father Thomas's masses, and the child has recently started to mimic the priest's gestures and repeatedly makes the sign of the cross.

—What's she doing? Anna asks.

—She's expressing herself with her body, I say. She mimics what she sees.

Anna laughs and I feel relieved. She doesn't look as worried as she sometimes has before. Our daughter laughs as well. The three of us laugh, the whole family.

—Good boy, Anna then says.

I find women a bit unpredictable. Somehow I thought it was only Mom who said things like that.

Sixty-three

I'm making great progress every time I use the gas cooker, although I'm still quite slow at cooking. In a short time I've managed to learn seven dishes: I can fry meat, both in slices and pieces, make two kinds of sauces, boil potatoes and various types of vegetables, boil rice, make meatballs, and, more recently, fry vegetables instead of boiling them. Then I can make various kinds of porridge for the child and have once tried to make rice pudding with cinnamon, which wasn't bad. I have to admit that it matters to me that Anna admires my genuine efforts to cook for her and her daughter.

I don't try anything complicated, mind you, like a whole bird or anything like that; Mom wasn't really into poultry. I've also popped in to see the woman in the restaurant a few times when I've forgotten myself in the garden and taken some of her cooked food home with me. I watch Anna when she's eating the woman's food, and I admit that it gives me satisfaction to hear that she doesn't praise it as much as mine.

The moment has come for me to attempt cooking fish. I go to the market with my daughter in the morning and try to choose something that bears some resemblance to the fish I'm familiar with back home, anything that more or less looks like haddock. There are several very small fish that I imagine might be from lakes and not the sea. You can't buy fish fillets either, just whole fish, complete with head, tail, bones, and all its innards. Despite all my experience of braving the elements at sea, I've honestly no experience of turning fish into those fillets in breadcrumbs you can just throw straight into the pan. But I soon give up trying to do it the way Mom used to; some of the ingredients just can't be found in this village, even though I've searched for them in all the shops, breadcrumbs, for example.

—What were you like as a child?

The question surprises me. Anna is constantly surprising me. We're finishing eating the small fish, which I ended up frying whole, and the mother and daughter sit opposite me at the table, waiting for my answer. Even though she might be wondering about me in relation to Flóra Sól, Anna's interest, nevertheless, seems to be genuine. Would I be on the right track if I told her I was redheaded and shied away from the sun, that I preferred a damp potato shed or shaded flower bed to being out in the sun? I was incredibly freckled as a child; my face was actually just the sum of its freckles. Dad has, of course, shown Anna the photograph collection, so the description shouldn't surprise her.

—I was short for my age, and when I was fourteen I was the smallest in my class, I say. Then I shot up one summer and was a head taller than everyone else my age when I was sixteen.

—So you changed into a fully grown man over one summer?

—Man might be a bit of an overstatement, overgrown teenager might be more like it. What about you, when did you become a woman? Or isn't that the kind of question a man asks a woman?

—It took a few summers, it happened gradually and effortlessly, without anyone ever really noticing it. I was one of the lucky ones.

Then she asks me if I've always been interested in plants.

—Yeah, pretty much from when I was a kid. Not exactly in the plants as such, not at first, it was more about being in the garden with Mom. My interest in the plants themselves came later. I started with a little flower bed south of the greenhouse, where I planted carrots and radishes and placed labels on them. I was seven years old and could see Mom through the glass clipping roses. Mom also experimented with all kinds of imported seeds and bulbs; the main thing that grew in my private flower bed, though, was weeds. I also used to read a fair bit as a child, lay out in the garden in the summer and sat in the greenhouse in the winter and read foreign books about children who had huts on tops of trees. I also went into the greenhouse later to study for my exams in the humidity, light, and heat. Even when there was snow, frost, and darkness outside, I'd run out into the greenhouse in my T-shirt with my books and trudge through the snow, knee-deep, with a pencil clenched between my teeth.

—Were you never teased about your hobby?

I ponder on how much I should tell Anna, what memories I should dig up from my past; one shouldn't reveal everything one's done.

—There was only one bad episode; I was ten years old and it was probably because of the color of my hair. They had been stalking me for several days, and I crunched mud with pebbles between my teeth while they rolled me over in the gravel and beat me up. I didn't feel bad after it, even though there was a taste of blood in my mouth and sand in my back teeth. One of them was forced to phone me that evening to apologize. Then he hung up without saying good-bye. I answered and the call was so short that Mom thought it was a wrong number.

—No, I say, what saved me was the fact that I was the best soccer player. They left you in peace then. I was like the other kids my age, although I didn't have the same urge to play soccer all day long.

Both girls listen to what I have to say with interest. The child's mother watches me as I'm talking, as if what I'm saying strikes a chord in her that she can understand.

Sixty-four

Anna is late and hasn't returned home from the library yet. It suddenly occurs to me that she might have met someone in the village and gone to the café with him, that the guy on the library steps might be delaying her. I can easily imagine her being accosted by a man, one of those guys who has been ogling her on the streets, inventing some excuse, and because she's so good and kind or spaced-out even, she might sit with him at the café. She'll only stop for a bit, she'll say, because she's rushing home, but because he's such a smooth talker he might make her forget her genetics and also make her laugh and forget what time it is.

So when she appears in the doorway five minutes later, slightly drenched from the rain, and with a box of cakes from the bakery in her arms, I'm unable to hide how delighted I am. I'm totally astounded by how absurdly thrilled I am, as if I were discovering her for the first time. She hands me the cakes and I find myself saying that she's in a nice sweater, although, of course, it's the same green sweater that she was in at the breakfast table. Then I suddenly grow insecure and burst into a blush and, even worse, she blushes, too. I feel uneasy and, to switch topics, offer to go downstairs to the laundry room and wash some of her clothes in the machine for her since I need to wash my working clothes.

—Since I have to do a wash for Flóra Sól anyway, I add as nonchalantly as possible, regretting it as soon as I've said it.

She looks somewhere between surprised and relieved.

—OK, she says. Can it be both whites and colors?

—Yeah, both. I can do two loads.

I haven't a clue of what I'm getting myself into. I could have washed the kid's tiny things in the sink.

—Can it be underwear as well or just jeans and T-shirts? she asks from the room.

—Underwear is fine, too. Do you mind if I wash your clothes with mine?

There's no turning back after this.

I first put the girls' laundry into one machine, and then I throw my working clothes into the second load. It takes me a hell of a long time to read the instructions and figure out how the machine works. When I've finished washing, I carry the wet laundry upstairs, clutching it in my arms, and hang it on the washing lines stretched over the balcony. Here I stand in a white T-shirt with clothes pegs between my teeth, just a few yards away from the old pensioner on the other side of the street, who hangs around home in his vest all day. I first hang up my daughter's leggings and then her mother's panties, so that, bit by bit, I'm putting my private life on the line, like the bloodstained sheets that used to be hung on balconies on wedding nights in the olden days. The old man watches me in eager anticipation, as I expose my temporary family life to the eyes of the world. No one should jump to any rash conclusions, though, just because I'm trying to make my child's mother's life easier by cooking for her while she researches her thesis in my rented apartment.

Sixty-five

Once a week there is a food market in the village, which all the farmers in the area bring their produce to. Sometimes there is also walking livestock, especially hens and other feathered creatures, so I grab the opportunity to take my daughter to see them. The market resounds with voices, bustle, and the cold smell of blood.

—Twi, twi, says the child, pointing at the bloody poultry hanging over our heads.

Just as I'm standing there under the plucked hens, I have a flashback of part of a dream I had last night. In the dream I was shooting a wild bird, although I'm far from being a hunter by nature. I doubt if I could kill an animal, I certainly couldn't kill any young ones, but if the animal were a fully-grown male animal and the purpose were to feed my family—I'm now reasoning like the father of a family—then there's a chance that I might kill it fearlessly and even look my prey in the eye. The dream might have something to do with the inner nature of man, Mom would say, with a mysterious air. So I still have Mom by my side to chat and discuss my dreams with.

We move farther into the section where the hares and rabbits are hanging, and I push the stroller through a forest of animals. My daughter leans against the back of the stroller to gain a better view of the hares dangling over her with their drooping heads. They don't seem to have planned for any tall guests at this market, so I have to stoop under the hairy ears.

I'm not thinking of anything in particular, which is when I'm struck by this preposterous idea, which comes to me like a cat lying on its back with its rubbery pink paws in the air, begging for its belly to be stroked. All of a sudden I can easily see myself as a married man, getting married even, in a church, and see that being with the same woman for the whole of one's life might be a goal worth pursuing, not necessarily to do anything in particular, but just to be in the same room as her. I'd be willing to bathe the child, change diapers, and have her in her pajamas when her mom came home from the research institute. Then I'd rub almond oil into my daughter's rosy cheeks so that when she was kissed, my wife would smell the almond oil on her. Then one of us would walk behind the other's coffin. Unless, of course, we both departed at the same moment, like that couple on the country road; there would be rain and mist on the windshield, and I would be on the point of turning the fan on full blast when, at the same moment, a truck would swerve onto the highway.

I see the trader talking to me, but don't immediately hear his words.

—Do you want the bigger one or the smaller one? he asks, daddy hare or mammy hare? He is holding the hooked pole he uses to take down the hare carcasses when customers request it. Flóra Sól is all eyes as he yanks the hairy animal off the hook.

—Oh, oh, she says when she sees the animal isn't moving.

I'm so absorbed in my own uncensored and premature fantasies about marriage that I'm seriously thinking of buying a hare. My gastronomic skills are far from being good enough to be able to handle anything as complex as that, though.

But the trader categorically affirms that it's easy to cook.

—A two-year-old could cook this blindfolded, he says, if I understood the dialect correctly. I suspect that might have a deeper meaning in the local vernacular.

He says he'll prepare the animal for me so that all I have to do is butter it with mustard and stick it in the oven.

—That's it, he says, with a very convincing air as he sharpens his knife.

—For how long?

—Between one to two hours, depending on when you get home, he answers, skinning the animal.

Two hours before dinner I unwrap the skinned violet animal enveloped in wax paper and start cooking. I follow the man's instructions to the letter and butter the animal with mustard both inside and out. But the thing that takes the longest is figuring out how the gas oven works. Because this is such an unfamiliar recipe I can't try out any adventurous side dishes. Instead I boil some potatoes and vegetables and make a red wine sauce, similar to the one I've made several times with the veal.

When I place the dish with the hare on the table, I sense my female friend is surprised by this evening's menu.

—Food smells good, she says, looking hesitantly at the meat. Is that rabbit?

—No, hare, I say.

My daughter is visibly excited and claps her hands.

—Twi, twi, she says, miming a bird with her hands.

—Our little harlequin, I say, wondering how I'm supposed to go about cutting the animal I've just cooked into consumable units. Anna saves me the bother and cuts the meat; then she cuts it even farther into tiny morsels for eight teeth.

The mustard hare isn't exactly bad, but it has a peculiar *bland* taste, that's exactly the way Anna words it.

—Special, she says, having a second helping, nonetheless. I think it's quite possible that Anna will eat anything that's put in front of her.

—I'm sorry for being so busy over the past weeks, she says. I haven't cooked anything since I got here. I'm no match for you, you're a fantastic cook. Where did you learn how to cook?

She's in a dress; this is the first time I've seen Anna in a dress. Our daughter is also in her yellow floral dress and best shoes and she's wearing a bib. They're both wearing hair clips and look as if they're celebrating something together. It occurs to me that Anna might have a birthday, that I know practically nothing about her, I don't even know when my child's mother's birthday is.

—No, she says, I had my birthday just before I came here, in April. There was just that kind of food smell in the air that made us decide to dress up for the occasion.

Sixty-six

Then I can't explain what happens next, no matter how many times I go over it in my head. As often as I'd fantasized about the possibility of this happening when I was alone, wrapped under the covers of the sofa bed in the living room, I just can't fathom what came over me. I'm inclined to think there was no thinking behind it at all.

Anna has washed up when I reenter the kitchen after putting our daughter to bed, and is picking up her toys. For once she isn't sitting with a book in front of her. She's in a dress with her hairclip and I sense she's looking at me in a new way, as if she had something personal to say to me. So I start to pull off my sweater and then unbutton my shirt and loosen my belt. As if I were going to bed or undressing for a doctor. There's nothing premeditated about it, in fact, I can't explain why I felt the time was ripe to strip off in the middle of the kitchen floor. She looks at me and I sense a kind of agitation in her when I start to undress out of the blue. In my mind I've already gone farther than her, gone the whole way, and I know as soon as I start taking my clothes off that I'm making a mistake. Nevertheless, I keep going, like a man who's got to complete an embarrassing but urgent task, until I'm standing there naked in the middle of a pile of clothes, a bird in its eider nest, an ostrich that has shed all its feathers. At the same moment I realize that Anna is holding a pen in her hand. It is only at that moment, and not before that moment, that the possibility dawns on me that she might have just intended to ask me to help her with some Latin terms in her genetics book, like a fellow pupil asking for some help with a Latin essay. Would a woman who had other intentions than scribbling notes into the margin of the book that is lying on the table—a woman who, let's just say for the sake of argument, wanted to make love to a man—be holding a pen in her hand? She looks at me exactly as if she had been on the point of asking me something about the genome and my response had taken her by complete surprise. Next she'll be asking the Latin genius:

—Do you know what this means? and stoop over the book to read out some tortuous Latin word in the text.

In any case, I'm stark naked, and rather than not do anything at all, I pick up the pile of clothes and dump it on the kitchen chair. Even though my predicament at this moment is a slightly awkward one, I nevertheless don't feel it's ludicrous. I'm fortunate enough not to take myself too seriously, not in that sense, not in the naked sense. I'm helped by the fact that my body is still somewhat alien to me. Nevertheless being a male can be tremendously embarrassing; I would sacrifice my entire plant collection including my last six-leaf clover just to know what she's thinking.

Instead of walking over to me and pointing out the word she doesn't understand, she smiles from ear to ear. I don't get women. It's the most beautiful smile in the world. Then she bursts into a giggle. I'm relieved. I laugh, too. Thank god I'm impervious to ridicule. Now that the body has made such a blunder of things, words have to take over, and as the sand rushes through the imaginary hourglass of my mind, I stumble to find the words to rescue myself. I'm terribly fond of Anna and don't want to lose her, I don't want this to make her leave. One word and everything's saved. One word and everything's lost. I'm hot. I'm cold. What words could be potent enough to delete this whole naked male body incident from her mind and to turn this situation around? Back to square one in my quest for the truth. No, I'm in the middle of a river with a powerful current sucking me into a vortex, and can't see the banks; I obviously haven't learned anything in my twenty-two years.

The best I can come up with is making another physical move. This time I bend over and choose one item from the pile. I first put on my underpants, then my T-shirt and loosely yank up my jeans without bothering to button up. Then I walk over to the sink, grab a kettle, and turn the tap.

—I better make some tea then, I say, filling the pot. I hear a slight tremor in my voice. I feel I need to make it up to her somehow, so that we can continue being friends, so that she can look at this as a mere digression, a totally freak incident. I glance at my watch, wishing I could rewind my life to six minutes earlier. How long does it take for a woman to forget something like this?

—All it needs is sleep and time, Mom would say.

If she were to suddenly start packing her things to go and write her thesis somewhere else, I would say without hesitation:

—Please don't leave.

I also wonder if a plant might change the situation. The idea of the plant comes to me automatically; what if I were to fetch the whole lily from the balcony ledge and give it to her, for example?

I look for the teabags.

—Do you know where the teabags are? I ask and my voice is back to normal again. I put the kettle on the gas stove and light it. My back is still turned to my child's mother and because I think she's still standing by the table, I channel my voice in that direction. Then she's suddenly standing right up against me, body to body, and I can feel the heat of the gas flames against my spine. She gently strokes my shoulder and then my elbow, sticking to the joints. Then she embraces me.

—Sorry about that, for laughing I mean, she says. I wasn't laughing at you, but just because I was so happy.

I hurriedly put the teapot down and turn off the gas and then follow her into the bedroom. I'm quicker than before, because my jeans are unfastened and I haven't buttoned up, and this time I do it without hesitation. I'm not even sure the velvet curtains are properly drawn; the evening sky peers through a gap, and a peculiar veil of pink cloud stretches across the horizon in a horizontal streak.

Sixty-seven

Once that's over I get the feeling that it's not over at all. There isn't a clear division between her body and mine yet, and for just a few minutes more we breathe in unison. In the ten minutes that follow I feel I couldn't be any closer to another human being. I feel it's incredible that I can be so close to a woman, that she's in me and I'm in her. I'm extremely fond of her and I think that the fact that we have a child together doesn't matter; she's new and different, the greenhouse has vanished into the mist of time, and I wouldn't be surprised if it had been attacked by vandals and smashed to pieces. It's all falling into place; Dad is very evasive when I ask him about how he's managing to give away the tomatoes.

I touch Anna all over, partly to convince myself that she's really all there. Afterward I walk out of the room to get a glass of water from the sink in the kitchen. The sky is strangely ablaze, and the moon drifts through the clouds. I see the old man opposite is having a sleepless night and stands at his window, staring at me. When I return to the bed I stroke her down her back, and she turns over without waking. She's so slim. Then I stroke her over her waistline, several times; her waist is just a few centimeters above the sheet. I grope my way forward like a blind man trying to find his way; her thigh is sticky. I do everything that occurs to me that I can do without waking her up. The sheet is crumpled on the floor but I leave it be. It's then that I realize that two eyes are staring at me through the darkness like two suns. Flóra Sól is standing up in her cot; she is puzzled that I'm not in my bed.

—Lie down and go to sleep, it's nighttime, I say, quashing any possibility of dialogue; changing her diaper is out of the question. But it's not very convincing, it's seven o'clock and a streak of daylight pierces through the window, but I long to have some peace with Anna; I don't want the child to disturb us. I have my eyes half closed to show her that I'm neither willing to talk nor play, but I can't see if she's offended by my refusal to engage with her. She sinks back into the cot again, helped by the force of gravity, and obediently lays her head on the pillow. I look at the horizontal row of three snaps on the back of her bodysuit and the quilt crumpled at her feet, so I creep over to spread it over her and glance fleetingly at her as I move. She's turned over to face the wall and is hugging her rabbit. Her lower lip is quivering; she's clearly fighting back some tears.

—We'll do the jigsaw tomorrow, I say. Good night, I add, to make her realize the conversation is over. I crawl back into the other bed and slip my arm around the woman lying beside me.

Ten minutes later my daughter is standing up in the cot again and looking at me in the dark.

—Da-da-da-da, she says in a rapid hush.

I sit up.

—Do you want us to go and make porridge? I ask.

I stand up, slip into my trousers, and stoop over the cot. My daughter releases the drenched ear of the rabbit from her mouth and smiles at me. My hands tremble as I pick her up and I realize that I'm full of new, unknown, feelings.

—We'll let Mammy sleep.

—Ma-ma dodo.

As I'm making the porridge, I try to work out this new situation that has developed and how I should behave when Anna wakes up and comes in. What am I supposed to do about this new intimacy? This is the first time that I've stayed put after sleeping with a girl. Up until now I've always vanished before they start making breakfast, not that I leave without saying good-bye. Besides, I couldn't leave; this is my apartment, which I'm renting, no more than Anna could leave, since we're both temporarily living under the same roof.

I throw the windows in the kitchen wide open. A thick mist hovers over the rose garden and it's dead still outside. The old man is no longer standing by the window; I imagine he must have taken a sleeping pill.

Sixty-eight

We've got eggs and milk, and if I borrow two cups of flour from my neighbor on the top floor, whom I can hear has been up for ages, I could make pancakes for Anna, using Mom's recipe book. In one of Father Thomas's movies there's a scene with people sitting at table eating pancakes with black currants and syrup; I think that combination could very well work.

I'm topless so I first slip on a T-shirt, and then hold Flóra Sól in her pajamas in my arms, walk up the stairs, and knock on the door. The old woman is glad to see us and invites us in, but I tell her we're pressed for time. She tells me her friend's asthma has been much better since she met the child and that the depression that plagued her with her asthma is also much better. The thing is that she's expecting a visit from her cousin from a neighboring town next weekend, a three-hour journey on the train; she's been through a lot and now she's got cancer. The question is whether she might be allowed to introduce the child to her cousin.

—She's taking the train straight back the next day, she says, as I shilly-shally uneasily in the doorway.

By the time my mistress comes in, all rosy-cheeked, I'm flipping my fourth pancake on the pan. She's holding a book in her arms with her hand stuck in so as not to lose the page. She acts as though nothing has happened and smiles at me and kisses her daughter, who is doing a jigsaw at the table; then she sits down and opens the book. We're platonic siblings again. Two individuals who accidentally had a little child with yellow angelic curls on her forehead.

—This is unbelievably good, she says of the syrupy pancakes.
I notice she has a scratched chin because of me. I don't know how
close I should be to her; we're once more separated by a table's
length. I'm not even sure that she notices that I'm looking at her,
watching her with new eyes. I don't see how I could ever have
thought that she was plain looking. My former self of a year and
a half ago is an obscure hidden mystery to me, like a stranger.

—What? she says with a smile. She almost seems shy.

—Nothing, I say.

I'm pondering on the miracle of being able to feel so close to
someone who isn't related to me. Then she asks:

—Were you operated on recently? You didn't have a scar
before, nineteen months ago.

Our daughter looks from parent to parent. Does she realize
that a new situation has now evolved in the house? That our relationship isn't just about her anymore?

—Yeah, I had to have my appendix out two months ago. I'm
not the same body that I was.

The child stares at me as I try to grab a hold of myself. I
suddenly find it difficult to handle this intimacy; it flusters me,
so I stand up and search for my sweater. I can't let Anna see
me in this condition, see how sensitive I am about her. She also
stands up.

—I'm off to the library, she says and kisses the child good-
bye. Then she hesitates a moment and looks at me. I hesitate and
look back at her as well; she's the one who takes the initiative and
kisses me.

This hurls me into a conundrum that I'm too agitated to deal
with, so I dress the child in her outdoor clothes and hold her in
my arms for the two flights of stairs down to the carriage. If Anna
were to ask me what my feelings are, what would I say? Should I
tell her the truth, that I'm not sure and that I'm thinking things

over? A man can't always express instant opinions on things the moment they happen.

There aren't many people around at this hour of the morning, but the three tables have been put up outside the café. I can't quite imagine what will happen next, whether the various parts of the day will be different from now on. How will the hours of the day be spread after last night? Will each part of the day, the morning, afternoon, evening, and night, take on a new meaning? Am I in a relationship or am I not in a relationship? Am I her boyfriend now or are we not a couple? Is this a love relationship or a sexual relationship? If we are a couple, should I be wondering if that makes me the father of a family, at the age of twenty-two? Or am I a friend she sleeps with and, if so, what's the difference?

Sixty-nine

I start off my rounds by hopping into the phone booth to call Dad. I let my daughter sit up in the stroller so that she can see me and jam my foot in the door of the phone booth. Dad is happy to hear me and starts by telling me that he's more relaxed even when he doesn't hear from me for several days now; he's not was as worried about me as he was before.

—Sorry I haven't called you for such a long time, I say.

—I can fully understand that you don't have as much need for your old man as you did before, he says. Then he changes subject; he's got some home news for me:

—Your twin Jósef has found a girlfriend at the community home.

—A nice girl, he adds, they live in the same home, he's going to bring her for a visit next weekend. Her parents are coming, too, so I was wondering what I should cook? I'm not very good at that stuff; your mother was the one who dealt with the cooking.

—How about fish balls? And cocoa soup with whipped cream for dessert, just like you made for me on my last night?

—That's a thought. Wasn't it two tablespoons of potato flour in the fish balls?

—As far as I can remember.

—What do you think of Ravel?

—Why do you ask?

—I've just been listening to him.

—I'm not sure he's the in-thing nowadays, Dad.

—You're not short of money, Lobbi, now that there are more of you in your home?

—No, no need to worry about that.

There's a mass going on in the church and it occurs to me that we could say hi to Father Thomas afterward, so I wait for him to come out of the church. He is happy to see me and wants to offer me an espresso and Amaretto at the café. We walk across the square together and I accept the coffee but turn down the liqueur. I take the child out of the stroller, hand her a biscuit, and sit opposite the priest, who is on nodding terms with everyone in the place. He looks at the child as we chat together, and I notice that he puts three lumps of sugar into his cup of coffee like my brother Jósef and eats the remains of the sugar with his teaspoon. Before I know it I've spilled out all my worries to Father Thomas, and tell him that I might have developed a crush on the woman I accidentally had a child with.

—I was so afraid that I would be rejected, that she would push me away from her, and when she didn't do that I became even more scared.

He finishes his cup while I explain to him what it's like to stand with one foot on a wobbling skiff and the other on a pier and to feel the pull of each foot going in opposite directions. I feel the need to fill him in on the background story and explain to him how a moment's carelessness with a kind of a friend of a friend can accidentally lead to a child, how this little person who is now holding a semi-soggy biscuit in her hand came by pure chance and now lives a life of her own.

—Stuff happens, I say, feeding some biscuit crumbs to two doves prowling around the table.

—Coincidences have a meaning, he says, ordering another espresso.

Once more I watch him take three sugar cubes out of the bowl and put them into his cup.

—You did things in a slightly different order than usual, he continues, you first had a child and then got to know each other, he says, sipping his coffee.

—How long can a love relationship last? And a sexual relationship? And a mixture of the two? Can that last a whole lifetime, forever?

—Yes, yes, it most certainly can, says Father Thomas. There are so many facets to a relationship between a man and a woman and it isn't for outsiders to understand what's going on between them.

I feel I can hear Mom's voice; that's exactly how she might have put it.

—It's so difficult to know where you have another person, to know what her feelings are, I say.

—Yes, that can happen, says Father Thomas, ordering another tumbler of Amaretto. As far as I can make out, you've already done all the things I would have advised you to give more thought to until you were sure.

My daughter has finished her biscuit and her face is totally smudged. I search my pockets and the stroller for something to wipe her with. My companion is quicker than I am and hands me a handkerchief.

—It's clean, he says, I keep it especially for the parish children, in case the need arises, he adds, smiling at the child. I can see that he's trying to work out what film to recommend. My daughter has developed an interest in the doves.

—I'm thinking of a movie, he then says, an old movie with, if I remember correctly, Yves Montana and Romy Schneider that I saw not so long ago and that might be instructive for you to watch. As you were saying, he continues, summarizing what I never said in just a few words, it isn't the first night that's the dangerous one, but the second night when the magic of the unknown has disappeared but not the magic of the unexpected. I think it was Romy who said it. You're welcome to pop over tonight and watch it, if you have a babysitter.

I put the hood on the child, shake his hand, thank him for the coffee, and tell him that it's unlikely that I'll be free in the evening. The big question that looms over me all day is whether we'll be getting into the same bed again tonight or whether that was just an isolated incident, an exception that had occurred under special circumstances last night, and the mother of my child might even have been trying to save me from an embarrassing situation. Up until now I've never slept with the same woman for two nights in a row because that would have meant that it had turned into a serious relationship and that commitments had been made. Although, mathematically speaking, last night was our second night together, it's a matter of opinion when one should start counting, whether it really was the second time or whether tonight should be counted as the second time.

Seventy

When Anna comes home from the library she's holding two bags. I notice her quickly checking and adjusting herself in the mirror in the hall before she puts the bags up on the kitchen table.

—I bought some food, she says, as I help her unpack the bags and arrange the shopping on the table. I want to slip my arms around her but feel this isn't the right moment. I see that she's bought some kind of fowl, probably duck, and different types of trimmings that I haven't a clue of how to cook. She says she's going to do the cooking herself.

—For a change, she says. I decided to pull up my socks and celebrate the fact that Flóra Sól and I have been with you for three weeks.

—Can you cook? I ask. I'm stunned. I thought that this girl— my child's mother—couldn't cook. I thought you were a geneticist, I say.

She laughs.

—Sorry, she says, for not cooking for you before, sorry for always letting you do it.

I hold my daughter in my arms and we watch her mother handling the bird like a person who knows what she's doing, confidently chopping dates, apples, nuts, and celery and diligently shoving the stuffing into the animal, all in the space of a few minutes, as if she had a long history of working in a restaurant kitchen behind her. I can't quite say whether I'm happy or disappointed to discover this new side to Anna. I was starting to enjoy cooking, even though I am still quite slow at it.

—I was brought up by a father who enjoyed nothing more than cooking and spent long hours in the kitchen trying to create new recipes, she explains. If he wasn't fishing trout, he was out hunting for ptarmigan; if he wasn't shooting ptarmigan, he was shooting geese or reindeer. One day he came home with common snipe and another with a whooper swan, which he said he'd shot by accident. I remember he spent all day cooking the swan with the kitchen door closed, and the swan filled the whole oven. But personally I soon lost interest in cooking. Besides, there wasn't any room for me in the kitchen. But once you've seen how it's done, it's no big deal, she says, stitching up the stuffed duck on the draining board so that the filling doesn't leak out. As I watch her make carrot mousse and sweet brown potatoes on the pan, I realize how I literally know nothing about the mother of my child, not even about the hunting interests of my child's grandfather.

—What? she asks and smiles at me.

—Nothing.

—Yeah, what? she says again. Why are you looking at me?

—I'm trying to work out what kind of a person the daughter of a ptarmigan hunter is.

—Deep inside? she asks, looking at me with her aquamarine eyes.

While the duck is in the oven I walk all the way down to the car to get the box with the remainder of the wine bottles. On the way up I meet Father Thomas and grab the opportunity to hand him two bottles.

—To be compared with your own production, I say. He tells me that they're all happy to have me back in the garden after my brief absence and that the monks are showing more interest in the garden than they did before.

—They're spending more time outside, he says, and they're realizing that it's good for them to get some fresh air. Brother

Paul tried to water a few flower beds and got his feet wet for the first time in twenty years, but was grateful to be back in touch with Mother Nature again. They're also all very happy about the way you've marked the roses. Now one can walk down the rose garden's old paths again and practice one's Latin by reading the names of the plants on the labels.

When I get back to the apartment, Anna has placed the side dishes on the table and is taking the duck out of the oven. Flóra Sól sits ready in her chair with her bib on and a spoon in her hand. It's got to be said, the food is delicious, but neither of us has much appetite. I admit I don't want to sleep on the sofa bed anymore, not when there are two places in the bed in the next room. When I'm about to stand up to bathe Flóra Sól and put her to bed, Anna halts me and says:

—I'll do it.

Looking out into the darkness through the kitchen window, I make out some lights in several windows of the monastery up on the hill. Tomorrow I'll mow the lawns and take the garden benches out of the storage room and give them a coat of oil. Then I'll sow various types of salad in the new beds and continue to work on the patches of spices.

I finish clearing up inside and walk straight into the bedroom, get into bed, and gently pull the quilt off Anna.

By the time Flóra Sól wakes up in the morning and stands up on the cot, we haven't slept much. I won't deny that I've started to think of the world like this: there's the two of us, then the others. Sometimes I feel the child is in our group, and the two of us and the child are one, and sometimes I feel the child belongs to the group with the others.

❈

Seventy-one

Although we haven't said a single word about our relationship, I'm nevertheless acquiring my first experience of being a couple with a child. Living with another person is no hassle at all, as long as you can make love to them. Even though my position isn't exactly clear, I'm still happy and excited, although I wouldn't exactly say that to anyone in those words out loud.

Anna is still immersed in her books and still lost in her thoughts, as if she were both present and distant at the same time. Except in bed, she's not distant there. Sometimes it's as if she doesn't notice me until we're both in bed. Then everything changes. Another life takes over once we're under the sheets; outside it, during the day, we're more like brother and sister. We've even been asked on the street if we were siblings. We don't hold hands on the street; we don't kiss during the day. We're like siblings when we take a stroll with the child or sit opposite each other with her, eating the dinners that we cook in turn. I've become more audacious than I was in my cooking, and because I really want to surprise Anna, I give in to my butcher and buy something he recommends: deer fillets.

Still, the night has started to contaminate the day, and the effects of what we get up to after hours stretch into the day. We're more hesitant and shy and talk less together during the day than we did before, because we're thinking about what's in store for the night. Sometimes I start thinking of the night straight after lunch and actually spend the whole day looking forward to going to bed.

In fact, we only really talk about things that are related to the child, although Anna still praises my cooking when I do it. I don't have much appetite in the evenings myself, but Anna always eats well. Neither of us makes any reference to what we are about to do, and we're both equally fast at bathing the child and tidying up.

Our daughter does us the favor of falling asleep as soon as her head hits the pillow. She sucks her pacifier with her rabbit beside her on the cushion and, a few moments later, dozes off. The child is perfect in every area, all day long. When I come back in, once Flóra Sól is asleep, Anna slams her book closed and stands up. We pay no heed to the fact that it's only eight o'clock and drop everything we have, books and clothes, and move to the bed without saying a word. There's nothing to disturb us; we've no television, no news of wars and men slaughtering each other, and we get no visits either, so we can speed up our daughter's dinnertime and putting her to bed; she doesn't mind. Sometimes we're in more of a hurry and we just leave the dishes on the table until the next day. The bed is a world of its own, where external laws don't apply. We're increasingly sparse in our use of words; you don't have to be able to express everything in words either. I can hear the priest's voice, and white subtitles appear on the ceiling, twenty feet above the bed, across the wings of the dove:

The longing in this case relates a great deal to the flesh.

Seventy-two

My daughter is having her afternoon nap and I'm standing in front of my lover who is reading at the table. She immediately puts her book down.

My intention was to tell her that I'm going up to the garden, but I surprise myself by saying something completely different:

—I was wondering if we could have a talk. About us.

—What do you mean about us?

—If we could discuss the status of our relationship.

She seems surprised.

—What status?

She says this in a low voice, averting her gaze. She's still holding the pen. That means that she hasn't stopped doing what she was doing before I interrupted her; she's just going to pause briefly to answer one or two questions. In the evenings she puts her pen down as soon as I've put the child to sleep. But not now. She's not ready to discuss our relationship, it's not the time, I was too quick, I didn't choose the right moment. Actually, I've very little to say about the matter myself.

—We sleep together.

There's a vast chasm between what I'm saying and what I'm thinking.

—Yes?

I shut up.

—You mustn't fall in love with me, she says finally, I don't know if I could live up to it.

I don't tell her that it's too late for that.

—You can't rely on feelings lasting forever, she says.

I'm trying to figure out what she means by feelings not lasting forever. To be honest, I have, in fact, started to wonder whether it might be possible to live like this for the rest of my life, and look forward to climbing into bed with the same woman every night. In fifty-five years' time I'll be as old as Dad is now, seventy-seven. Another fifty years would mean approximately another eighteen thousand two hundred fifty evenings and nights with the same woman. That's provided there's no car accident in a beautiful lava field. That means eighteen thousand two hundred fifty nights to rejoice over and look forward to. I glance at the clock and see a way of turning this situation around for me, around for us.

—Anyway I was just wondering if we should go to bed, I say, as if to wrap up a matter that can't be settled in any other way. It's two p.m. and our daughter has about another hour to go in her siesta.

This is where most of our attempts at conversation end, in bed precisely, although you can't really say that we've settled anything. But somehow there's never any need to discuss the matter any further after that. Physical contact manages to lay all outstanding issues to rest, and the problem evaporates like that redblue mist over the hills after the first mass of the day.

Anna later calls me from the doorway to the bedroom so I look up. I don't notice the camera until she's pressed the click and the flash goes off in my face, as I'm half buried under my quilt. She winds the camera.

Up until now she hasn't taken many pictures of Flóra Sól outdoors.

—I wanted to have a picture of you, as a memento.

—Are you leaving? I feel like she might as well be pointing a gun at me and not a camera. I briskly look death in the eye, right before the shot is fired. I could easily have said: Go ahead, shoot me then.

—No, she says. Finished.

I try to hide my mental turmoil by getting out of bed and slipping into my trousers. But I'm careful not to turn my back on Anna, my lover.

Seventy-three

I'd be willing to share my experiences with someone, and yet I'm not the type of guy to divulge what's going on between a woman and me to someone else. When someone is frank with you and tells you something a bit personal, you can't go around telling anyone about it. What happens between Anna and me is between her and me. But I don't feel I'm betraying her trust by popping in to consult the expert on divine love in room seven of the guesthouse. I'm helped by the fact that I've acquired more experience in various areas since I last discussed issues related to this with him some ten days ago.

I sit with my daughter, wriggling on my knees in her striped stockings, while we talk together; and because I'm visiting Father Thomas on a formal matter, my daughter and I sit on one side of the desk and the priest on the other. He offers me a shot, but I don't think it's appropriate for me to be drinking when I'm with the child. I notice a porcelain doll in a blue knitted dress has been placed on the middle of the desk. I get straight to the point.

—How does a man know if a woman loves him?

—It's difficult to be certain about anything when it comes to love, says the priest, pushing the doll toward my daughter.

—What if the woman says she's scared you won't come back when you go out to the shop?

—Then it could be that she is the one who actually wants to leave, alone.

I notice him observing the child playing as he's talking to me.

—And when a woman is miles away in her thoughts, does that mean she's not keen?

—It can both mean that and mean that she is keen.

—But if a woman tells a man that he can't fall in love with her?

—That can mean that she loves him. It reminds me of an old Italian film that you might like to watch, which deals with similar problems. The director shows little faith in dialogue as a means of settling feelings.

—But if she says she's not ready for a relationship?

My daughter hands me the doll; she wants me to take its knitted dress off.

—That could mean that she is ready but doesn't know if you're ready and is afraid you might reject her.

—But if she says she wants to go away and be alone?

—That could mean that she wants you to come with her.

The priest has stood up and is looking through his shelves.

—There's such a thing as wise love, as verse reminds us, he says from the other side of the room with his back turned to me, but there's no such thing as wise passion. But if life were solely to be based on wisdom, you'd miss out on the passion, as they say in here somewhere, he says, and I know he's not quoting from the Bible.

My daughter wants me to put the knitted dress back onto the doll again. Squeezing the arms into the sleeves takes the longest.

—There, he finally says, walking toward me with a tape in his hand. You can learn a lot about women's feelings by watching Antonioni. Have you got a video player yet?

Seventy-four

I sense a mounting restlessness in Anna. Yet everything seems normal on the surface. Even though she's behaving pretty much as she should, I suddenly feel I'm running out of time.

—What? she asks. You're staring at me so intensely and look all kinds of worried, and you've got that same accusing expression that Flóra Sól has when she's looking at me.

—Are you leaving? I ask as nonchalantly as I possibly can, but I feel my voice is trembling.

—Yes, she says.

To be honest, I was starting to believe that my hunch was groundless. But life has a habit of surprising you like that: when you're expecting something good, something bad happens; when you're expecting something bad, something good happens. I'm quoting from a movie, a boring western in this case that I saw before I started watching quality movies with the priest.

—When?

—The day after tomorrow. I've done as much as I could here; I've reached a conclusion.

I don't dare ask her what conclusion it is, whether it's linked to scientific research or our relationship, so I stick to film dialogue instead. I long to say to her that, if she's willing to give our relationship a chance, then everything might be different than she expected. Everything is crumbling inside me, but I don't let on.

—Sorry, she says softly. You're a wonderful guy, Arnljótur, kind and generous; it's just something with me, I'm so confused.

I feel dizzy, as if I'm losing touch with my surroundings, and my nose suddenly starts to bleed. I drag the stream of blood, like a red veil, behind me to the sink. I suck it up my nostrils, lean my head back, swallow the blood, and hold on to the edge of the sink. There's a torrent of blood, like some sacrificial ritual is taking place and an animal is being led to the slaughter.

Anna gets a wet cloth and helps me to wipe the blood off. She looks worried.

—Are you OK? she asks.

I sit down at the kitchen table and lean my head back. Anna stands on the floor in front of me; she's wearing a fuchsia sweater, a very special color I've never seen before.

—Are you absolutely sure you're OK? she asks again.

We're both silent; then looking down she hesitantly says:

—I feel there's so much I have to do before I become a mother.

I take the cloth away from my nose; it seems to have stopped bleeding. There's no point in me telling her that she already is a mother.

—I'm just not ready to have a child straight away, she says, as if we were still a childless couple planning our future. She's silent for a brief moment.

—I'm incredibly fond of you, but I just want to be alone—for a few years—and find myself and finish my degree. I feel I'm too young to found a family straight away, says the two-years-older genetics expert.

I clutch the cloth in my hand; it's red from the blood and there are splatters of red on my shirt, too.

—You and Flóra Sól get on so well, much better than I do, she adds. You immediately became so close and are always doing something fun together, and you've created this world for the two of you that I feel I'm not a part of. I mean, you're both left-handed, she swiftly adds.

—But she's just a kid.

—You always agree with each other.

—What do you mean?

—You even speak Latin together. I feel I'm one too many.

—It's a bit of an exaggeration to say she speaks Latin. She knows a few words, five or ten, I say, probably seven, I add after thinking it over a short moment. She just picked up a few words at the masses. Kids do things like that.

—Ten months old?

—Of course, I don't have any experience of other children.

—I don't get as much out of the mother role as you do out of the father role.

—Maybe I just wanted to attract your attention, to impress you.

—By teaching her Latin?

—By taking good care of her. And you, too, I say very softly.

—You're a great guy, Arnljótur, she repeats, good and intelligent. Then she says she's very fond of me.

—These forty days have been wonderful, she continues, but I can't expect you to hang around waiting for me, she says, burying her face in her hands, while I'm finding myself, I mean.

—No, I say, you can't. Still though, she could always try asking me to wait, I think to myself.

✳

Seventy-five

The last night is like a long and excessively slow memory. It's a blue night, and I move cautiously in the bed to avoid waking Anna. She's breathing deeply. I try to slow down my own breathing to bring it into sync with hers, without falling asleep myself. I'm right up against her, but no matter how tightly we lie together, there's an ocean between us because we're not one. I feel like I'm losing her like I lost Mom on the phone, like black sand running through my fingers, no, like a wave leaking through my fingers. And I'm left sitting there, licking my salty fingers.

I can't sleep a wink, but instead try to slow down time and devise something that will stop her from leaving. I can't lose Flóra Sól either. I feel like I have to guess something, anything really, to be able hold Anna back. I might unexpectedly get the right answer, like on those TV quizzes, and end up taking the jackpot home.

Hang on, hang on, hang on, I try to reason with myself. I feel like I'm in the middle of a swarm of crazy arctic terns, being assailed from all sides and unable to think of any way of protecting myself. Since I can't chain myself to her like a pacifist to a tank, it occurs to me that I could maybe show her some place she would be unable to resist and that would make her quickly change her mind.

She has to get the train at nine, but at seven she's still mine to hold, and I grope under the sheets, stalling the menace of the rising dawn. Day breaks through the curtains in the same violet as that of the skinned wild boar at the butcher's. Then she's suddenly awake and I haven't slept all night. She seems confused. Our daughter is still sleeping soundly.

—I had a really weird dream, she says. I dreamed your were in new blue boots with Flóra Sól in your arms and she was also in identical new blue boots, except they were tiny. You were in the rose garden but there was no other color in the dream, not even the roses, just the blue boots. Then I was suddenly in a narrow alley and I could see you going up a long stairway and disappearing behind a door. I knocked on the door and you answered with Flóra Sól in your arms and invited me in for tea.

Then it just blurts out of me without warning:

—Maybe we'll have another child together, later. I say this without daring to look at her.

—Yeah, she says. We might.

We both get out of bed. I'm standing right in front of the mirror and I take Anna's arm and gently tow her until we're both reflected in the mirror, like a studio family photograph, set in a carved gilded frame, as if we were formally acknowledging our forty days of cohabitation. I'm pale and skinny and she's pale, too. Our daughter stands behind us, having just woken up in her cot, and smiling from ear to ear, with her rosy cheeks and dimples on her elbows, so the whole family is in frame now.

—You can have Flóra Sól, she says suddenly in a low voice, as if she were reading a new script for the first time, as if she were trying to fit the words to the circumstances. She's looking me in the eye through the mirror.

I say nothing.

—When I see how well you get along and how responsible you are, then I know that I can leave her with you without any worries. Of course, I'll always be her mom, but you don't have to be worried about me turning up one day and taking her away from you. But I'll still help you bring her up as best I can. I'd do anything for her, she ends up saying.

—Sorry, she says finally. She kisses me. Give me six months, she ends up saying.

Seventy-six

Once we've had some bread with cheese, like school kids eating their picnic, sitting silently opposite each other and sharing an apple between us and the child, I stand up to clear away the breakfast while Anna gets her clothes and books together.

When she's ready and standing in the corridor, she locks me in an embrace and I think she must be able to feel my heartbeat, which fills the room and the buzz in my ears. Then she hugs the child; she doesn't want us to accompany her to the station. I've never been good at good-byes; I didn't even say good-bye to Mom.

I'm left sitting alone with the child, and I dress her. Then we sit over the gardening book together at the table and skim to my daughter's favorite chapter, the chapter on garden ponds and streams.

—Ma-ma, says the child.

—Yeah, Mammy will come back later.

We're looking at the streams when there is a knock on the door.

I immediately dash toward the door, glance in the mirror, and run a hand through my hair. It's my neighbor from upstairs. She's holding a large steaming dish, which she hands me without saying a word. I make out various types of fish, including shellfish and crab's claws, protruding from a base of beautiful yellow rice, baked tomatoes, and onion rings.

—I'll be straight back, she says and disappears up the stairs.

I hold the door ajar with my foot and see that Flóra Sól is following me at a distance on her little feet to see the guest. She stands in her knitted leggings and props herself up against the door beside me.

—Good girl, I say, and have both hands tied now as I stand in the doorway with a steaming dish.

Our neighbor quickly reappears with a cherry cake that she says is the dessert. Her face radiates when she sees the child, and she swiftly puts the cake down on the kitchen table so that she can greet her. Flóra Sól is happy with the visit, too; we never have guests. She lets go of the sash of the door and totters unassisted across the floor to get a date from a bowl on the table. Then she follows the same path with it back across the floor to the woman and hands it to her.

—I thought I might give you this because the young lady is gone, says the old woman. The child has to eat, even though Mammy's gone.

I thank the old woman for the food, for her warm heart, as I put it in her dialect, because I've been taking a look at the chapters on manners and customs. Still I'm slightly worried she might want to linger, since I was planning to take the child out to phone Dad.

When the old woman has finished her cup of tea, I put my daughter into her woolen coat with the double row of buttons and stitched pockets and outdoor shoes.

—Shall we ring Granddad Thórir?

—Gran-da.

I don't tell Dad Anna has left, and for once he doesn't even give her a single mention, nor does he give me a weather report, or his usual lowdown on the conditions of the roads and vegetation either. But there's a tension in him:

—I don't know how you're going to take what I'm about to tell you now.

—Have you met a woman?

—Have you turned psychic, boy? It's not as if I met her yes-terday, there was quite a prelude to it; she's an old friend of your mother's and mine.

—Well, you've mentioned Bogga every time I've called you; you've been doing the electric wiring for her and fixing her win-dows and she's been inviting you for meat soup and glazed ham.

—Bogga has asked me to move in with her; she lives alone in the house.

Then Dad hesitates a moment.

—I would have wanted to continue living here, but I feel I don't know how anything works without your mother.

Then he pauses before changing subject:

—How's your little Flóra doing?

—She's started to walk.

—And what about your rose garden?

—It's turning into the most beautiful rose garden in the world again.

—That's good to hear, Lobbi lad.

There's another silence before he tackles the next bit:

—I've been thinking things over and I see now that I've been putting unnecessary pressure on you about your studies. If you're happy, then so is your old man. Jósef is happy with his girlfriend, too, so I don't need to have worries about my boys.

—No, you don't have to have any worries about us.

—You know you still have your mother's inheritance if you want to travel the world and visit more gardens.

Once my daughter has said *Granda* down the phone and I've said good-bye to Dad, I go looking for the priest. I have to tell him that my situation has changed yet again, that it's just me and the child now, as it was supposed to be in the beginning anyway. We find Father Thomas in the guesthouse. I tell him Anna has left.

—Yeah, it isn't always easy to understand feelings, he says, patting me on the shoulder. Then he pats the child on the head.

—Things normally get worse before they get better again, he says when we're sitting opposite him at the desk. He moves the penholder so that it doesn't block his view of the child and fetches the porcelain doll in the knitted blue dress.

—When everything is over there's always some element that's been overlooked, just like with Christmas preparations, he says skimming through his collection on the shelves.

—As you can imagine, there is such a vast selection of films about the unpredictable paths of love that it would take me ages to find them all on these shelves.

My daughter is tired and rests her head on my shoulder. I stick the pacifier into her mouth. Then I notice that a small clay pot has appeared on the desk filled with soil and green shoots that barely peep over the edge. I don't ask about the species.

—Still though, if you give me a bit of time and pop in, say, this afternoon, I might have found some movies for you. I'd focus on some women directors, although they're not free of irony.

Then he switches topics and says that everyone in the monastery agrees that the garden is quite extraordinary. Although he doesn't go as far as to call it a miracle, the transformation is far more spectacular than anyone could have imagined, and from what Brother Zacharias and others have been able to gather from some of the old manuscripts, the garden is once more as it's described in the ancient books; its beauty equals the beauty of the heavenly mother of God.

—The eight circular rose groves around the pond elevate the garden to perfection, he says, arranging some papers on the desk.

—Yes, I say. My daughter has fallen asleep on my shoulder. I gently stroke her cheek.

—The monks can hardly bear the thought of being cooped up in the library with all that beauty within reach through the window now, he adds, leaning back in his chair and studying the sleeping child.

—People have been giving the monastery small donations, and we have a little bit of a fund, although it doesn't really compare to the wealth of former times, he says, smiling at me. Up until now it's mainly been used for the restoration of manuscripts, but we've agreed that it would be right to use a part of what has been collected to pay you a wage and for the maintenance of the garden. We've also thought of making the garden more accessible so that more than thirteen men can enjoy it, and even opening it up to tourists.

When I stand up with the sleeping child in my arms, he nods toward the flower pot with the frail green shoots and says:

—No, that's not your rose species; it's a future lily, if I read the writing on the packet of seeds correctly.

Father Thomas escorts us to the street; he probably isn't expecting me to return in the afternoon. I have the sleeping child in my arms. As he's shaking my hand to say good-bye, he suddenly asks:

—What's your rose called again, the one you moved into the garden?

—Eight-petaled rose.

—Yes, eight-petaled rose, of course, I thought so. You should take a look at the rose in the window over the altar in the church the next time you're passing; it has eight connate petals around its core.

✳

Seventy-seven

We wake up early in the morning; it's still dark outside. At some point in the night I lifted my daughter up into my bed and now she's sitting beside me, looking around and in the air. Her mother's scent still lingers in the quilt.

—Twi, twi, says the child, pointing at the dove with half a wing.

I turn to my daughter and she smiles from ear to ear.

—Shall we go home to Granddad?

—Gan-da.

—Does Flóra Sól want to walk on moss?

—Should Daddy pick crowberries for you?

—Does Flóra Sól want to try sitting on a tussock?

I carry her into the kitchen in her pajamas, fill the kettle, and light the gas. Then I put some oatmeal in the pot and tie a bib around the child while I wait for it to boil.

We don't linger much after breakfast, but get dressed and go out. I put the child in the carriage it isn't totally bright yet, and a peculiar reddish-blue mist hangs over the monastery in the still air.

When we get into the church I put the brakes on the carriage under the doomsday painting. I pick up my daughter, sit her on my shoulders, and we set off on a journey toward the sun, moving through the semidarkness at the very back of the church. We give ourselves plenty of time, stopping frequently on the way. I slip some coins into the jar for Saint Joseph and light a candle. I hold the burning candle with one hand and my child's ankle with the other, carefully trying to ensure that the wax doesn't leak. Slowly we move farther into the church toward the chancel where the sun is just rising, a flare of amber on the edge of dawn. Bit by bit, the delicate light narrows into a beam through the stained-glass window, filling the church like a shaft of translucent white cotton. My daughter remains perfectly still on my shoulders, and shielding my eyes with my hand, I look into the light, into the blinding glare; and then I see it, way at the top of the chancel window, the violet-red eight-petaled rose, just as the ray pierces through the crown and lands on the child's cheek.

About the Author

Audur Ava Olafsdottir was born in Reykjavík, Iceland, in 1958. She studied art history and art theory in Paris and is a lecturer in history of art at the University of Iceland and a director of the University of Iceland Art Collection. She has curated art exhibitions in Iceland and abroad, for example, at the Venice Biennale, and written about art and art history in various media.

Audur Ava is the author of three novels, a book of poetry, and a play. The first novel, *Raised Earth*, was published in 1998. *Rain in November* was published to rave reviews in 2004 and received the City of Reykjavik Literary Award. *The Greenhouse*, published in 2007, won the DV Culture Award for literature and a women's literary prize in Iceland and was nominated for the Nordic Council Literature Award. Since *The Greenhouse* was published in France in the autumn of 2010 under the title of *Rosa Candida*, the book has attracted a great deal of coverage in the French media and received unanimously good reviews. In September 2010, it received the *Prix de Page* literary award as the best European novel of 2010. The *Prix de Page* award is determined by a group of 771 bookstores in France where the book was on the best-seller's list for five consecutive months. The novel was also nominated for three other literary awards in France, including the prestigious *Femina* award. In January *The*

Greenhouse won the Canadian *2011 Prix des libraires du Québec* award. Audur Ava Olafsdottir published *The Hymn of Glitter*, a book of poetry, in 2010, and her first play will premiere at the National Theatre of Iceland in September 2011.

Audur Ava Olafsdottir's middle name, Ava, was adopted a few years ago as a tribute to the blind medieval French saint, Ava. Audur Ava Olafsdottir lives and works in Reykjavik.

About the Translator

As a translator and playwright, Brian FitzGibbon has a particular passion for the translation of fiction. With experience that spans over twenty years, he has translated a vast array of film scripts, treatments, stage plays, and novels, working exclusively into English from Italian, French, and Icelandic.

His translation of the Icelandic cult novel *101 Reykjavik* by Hallgrimur Helgason, published by Faber & Faber in the United Kingdom and Scribner in the United States in 2002, was hailed by the *Guardian* as "dazzling" and the *New York Times* as "lucid."

Brian's one-act play, *The Papar*, was staged by the Abbey Theatre at the Peacock in Dublin in 1997, and subsequently adapted into a short film called *Stranded*, premiered at the Tribeca Film Center in New York one year later. An Icelandic translation of the play was broadcast on Icelandic radio in 2005 and nominated for a Gríman Award the same year.

His full-length play, *Another Man*, was a finalist at the Playwrights Slam at the 2005 Chichester Theatre Festival in the United Kingdom. A radio adaptation of the play was broadcast on Icelandic State radio in the spring of 2008 and nominated for an Icelandic Gríman Award.

✳